BOTANY LESSON

Skip opened two bottles of pop, handed Deidre one, and climbed back up front with his. "Say, look at that crazy tree over there, Mr. Carpenter!"

It was indeed a crazy tree. It had a tail and a big head. And pointed teeth. It was sunning itself in the slanted morning sunlight. It was watching Sam.

A big glob of saliva ran out of the corner of the tyrannosaur's mouth and dropped with an almost audible plop to the ground. It roared. Or screamed. It was difficult to tell which.

"Let's get out of here!" Skip whispered...

Also by Robert F. Young
Published by Ballantine Books:

THE LAST YGGDRASILL

ERIDAHN

ROBERT F. YOUNG

A Del Rey Book

BALLANTINE BOOKS • NEW YORK

A Del Rey Book

Published by Ballantine Books

Based on the novelette "When Time Was New," copyright © 1964 by The Galaxy Publishing Corporation for *If* Magazine, December 1964.

Library of Congress Catalog Card Number: 82-91038

ISBN 0-345-30854-9

Manufactured in the United States of America

First Edition: June 1983

Cover art by Darrell K. Sweet

To Reggie,
Bonnie,
Eddie,
Mel, and Billy

_____Chapter

_____1

THE YOUNG ANATOSAUR standing beneath the ginkgo tree didn't startle Carpenter, but he was dumbfounded when he saw two kids sitting in the tree's branches. Since he was in the Age of Reptiles it was only natural that he should meet up with a dinosaur, but it wasn't in the least natural that he should meet up with a girl and a boy. What in the name of all that was Mesozoic were they doing in the Upper Cretaceous Period?

He leaned forward in the driver's seat of his battery-powered triceratank and stared up into the tree's branches through the reptivehicle's unbreakable windshield, which, from without, was indistinguishable from the reptivehicle's head. No, the kids weren't an illusion. They were as real as the anatosaur that had treed them. And they were scared: Their faces were as white as the distant chalklike cliffs that showed to the north above

1

the scattered stands of willows, live oaks, cycads, and ginkgoes that patterned the Cretaceous plain.

Suddenly it dawned on him that they must be connected in some way with the anachronistic fossil whose origin he had come back in time to investigate. Miss Sands, the North American Paleontological Society's new chronologist, had not spotted them when she timescoped the area, but she could hardly have been expected to, for timescopes could not pick up anything smaller than a sauropod or a hill. The reason he had been taken unawares was that he had failed to think one inch beyond the end of his nose. Simple logic should have told him that if, as the fossil indicated, there were human beings living somewhere in the region, some of them were bound to have children.

The anatosaur was standing on its hind legs, chewing on the lower leaves of the ginkgo tree. Probably it had forgotten all about the two kids it had chased into the branches. But the two kids had not forgotten it, and the appearance of the triceratank, which looked exactly like a ceratopsian of the genus *Triceratops elatus*, had doubled their fright.

As yet unaware of the mechanical monster creeping up behind it, the anatosaur continued to chomp away with its duck-billed jaws. It was big and fat and flat-headed, with large and powerful lower limbs and much shorter upper ones. It had a long, ponderous tail whose primary purpose was to balance it when it walked. Its skin was muddy brown in color. It was not carnivorous and probably had chased the kids up the tree merely because they happened to be in its way.

"Come on, Sam," Carpenter said, addressing the triceratank by nickname, "let's teach it some manners!"

Since emerging from the photon tunnel, NAPS' big Llonka time machine had drilled down through the eras, he had been traveling in a northerly direction, maintaining a snail's pace and looking for some sign of human life. One of the reasons he had failed at first to tie the children in with the fossil was that it consisted of the petrified skeleton of an adult modern man and had led him to think in terms of adults. But the fact that there was only one such skeleton had not led him to think there was only one anachronistic resident of the Upper Cretaceous. In order to have your bones preserved for posterity, you have to be buried in terrain that will not destroy them, and it followed logically that if a human inhabitant of Cretaceous-16—NAPS' official designation of the area—had been buried in such a way, whether by accident or design, there were other such inhabitants who had not been.

Throwing Sam into higher gear, he sent a charge from the right upper horn-howitzer zooming past the anatosaur's left hip. The charge struck a nearby cycad, emitted a big bang, and broke the cycad in two. The anatosaur gawked at the broken tree, then, hearing Sam's approach, twisted its head around. One look at the charging triceratank was enough to send the animal barreling off in the direction of a stand of willows, its tail stretched straight behind it.

Carpenter brought the big reptivehicle to a halt several yards from the ginkgo's trunk and looked up at the two kids again. Their faces had turned from chalk white to gray. The anatosaur had been bad enough, but now they were apparently threatened by an awesome four-legged, three-horned creature with a countenance capable of scaring all the denizens of C-16, with the glaring exception of *Tyrannosaurus rex*, out of their wits.

Carpenter slid across the driver's seat and opened the passenger-side door. Hot and humid but incredibly fresh air rushed into Sam's air-conditioned interior. He jumped down to the ground, his red plaid shirt, brown trousers, and black boots striking a discordant note in the Cretaceous concerto of times past. The ginkgo stood all by itself on a slight rise. The plain encompassing it extended northward to the chalk-white cliffs, westward to wooded highlands beyond which young mountains rose, eastward to the inland sea that was hidden by numerous stands of trees, and southward to a wide river near whose northern banks the photon field of his entry point was located.

"Come on down, you two. Sam won't hurt you."

Two pairs of the widest, bluest eyes he had ever seen focused on his face. The amazement filling them was unleavened by even a particle of understanding.

"I said come on down," he repeated, beckoning to them. "There's nothing to be afraid of."

The girl and the boy faced each other and began talking in a strange tongue. At length they reached a decision, left their aerie, and shinned down the trunk. They stood there with their backs against it, looking at him.

He walked toward them, halted several feet away. The boy was about nine, the girl about eleven. The boy was wearing a dark-blue short-sleeve blouse with gold piping and trousers to match. The girl was similarly clad, except that her garments were azure and her trousers more like pantaloons. It was hard to tell which outfit was the more disheveled. The girl's appeared dirtier, probably because of its lighter color. Both pairs of boots were caked with mud. The girl was about an inch taller than the boy. She stood very straight, and she had buttercup-color hair that fell to her shoulders. The boy's hair was darker and cut short. Both kids had delicate features, and both were thin. Carpenter had a hunch they were brother and sister.

At length the boy, gazing earnestly into Carpenter's gray eyes, gave voice to a series of phrases. Carpenter shook his head, and the boy spoke in what seemed to be another tongue. Carpenter shook his head again. He spoke to the boy in English, then in French and German, the only other modern languages he was familiar with. Each time the boy shook his head. The girl as yet had not said anything. She just stood there, regarding Carpenter stonily.

He did not try any of the ancient languages he was acquainted with. Modern kids were not apt to be familiar with Aramaic or Ionic or Doric Greek—languages he had studied when pasttripping for NAPS' sister society, the Historical Investigating Association. For these *were* modern kids. They had "modern kids" written all over them. He had no idea what modern country they were from, or how they had happened to wind up in C-16, but they must have come back via a Llonka time machine, and it was highly unlikely they had come back alone.

All seemed lost insofar as communication was concerned, but this did not prove to be the case. The boy dug into one of the pockets of his trousers and pulled out what appeared to be two pairs of earrings. He attached one pair to his earlobes and handed the other to Carpenter, indicating for him to attach them to his. The rings were tiny pendants with clamps attached to them. No, not pendants—diaphragms. The clamps were self-adhesive and the diaphragms fitted within Carpenter's ear openings without interfering with his hearing.

The boy turned to the girl. "Come on, Deidre," he said in

English, "you've got a pair with you. More than one. I know you have. Put them on."

Deidre? Well, anyway, the name had sounded like Deidre. The girl pulled out an identical pair of earrings from a pocket in her blouse and attached them to her earlobes. But she had yet to say a word.

Carpenter had a hunch he was being conned. "I must say," he told the boy drily, "you caught onto my language real fast."

The boy shook his head. "No, I'm still speaking my own," he said, and Carpenter saw that his lip movements weren't synchronized with his words. "The hearrings only make it seem to be your language. They work in conjunction with a person's auditory nerves and effect an idiomatic translation. People's names, of course, aren't translatable, and are made to sound similar to names the hearer's familiar with. And some words just slip through as they are, because the hearrings aren't one hundred percent perfect. Anyway, now that both of us are wearing them, whatever I say to you sounds the way you would say it, and whatever you say to me sounds the way I would say it. On Mars we have such a medley of languages a single person could never learn them all. Even in individual countries there are many different tongues. So sooner or later hearrings had to be invented, and finally they were. Almost everybody carries at least two pair."

"Mars?"

"Yes. Mars is where we're from. Greater Mars. My name is Skip."

"What's your last name?"

The boy appeared puzzled. "People on Mars only have one name."

"My name's Jim Carpenter," Carpenter said. He looked at Deidre. She looked back at him, but in such a way that she seemed to be looking right through him. "Is she your sister?"

"Yes, sir."

"Doesn't she talk?"

"Well, you see, Mr. Carpenter, she can't talk to you. She's a princess."

"I see. Well, if she's a princess, that means you're a prince. And *you're* talking to me."

"Yes, but with me it's different. She's next in line for the throne of Greater Mars, and that makes her something special. And not only that," Skip added, "she's kind of conceited to begin with."

Deidre glared at him but said nothing.

"The reason we're here on Earth," Skip explained, "is that we were kidnapped."

So here I am, Carpenter thought, way back in the Upper Cretaceous, and whom do I rescue from the duck-billed jaws of an anatosaur but a princess of Mars and her younger brother, Skip! And now, it turns out, they were kidnapped!

But what Skip had told him probably was not any harder to believe than what he now proceeded to tell Skip and his sister. "I'm from Earth of the year A.D. 1998, which is 74,051,622 years from now." He pointed to the triceratank. "Sam over there is my van, although actually he's more like a tank than a van, and, to call a spade a spade, he's really an armored truck. Sam is his nickname. He has a big Camins engine which works off batteries that the engine keeps recharging, and he's equipped with a small photon diffusion unit that enables him to make limited jumpbacks in time. After he jumps back, he can return to when he was plus whatever time he spent in the past, but an inbuilt governor prevents him from jumping any farther into the future. He has automatic holo cameras concealed in his sides, and usually when I go back to prehistorical times I do so solely to make holo documentaries, but this time I came back for an additional reason: to find the origin of a human fossil. New techniques in dating have enabled paleontologists to pinpoint time periods with precise accuracy, and they can determine when whatever turned into a fossil died almost to within a week. But they can't tell exactly where it happened because of geological changes, in this particular case because of the Laramide Revolution."

Even Deidre's eyes had grown large. They made him think of autumn asters.

"Usually when I come back I don't come back alone," he went on, "but the holographer who was supposed to come with me quit, and I didn't want to wait for a replacement. I'm supposed to take holographs for two weeks. In case you kids don't know how a Llonka time machine works, it does so by diffusing light. Light is a sort of yardstick you measure time by, and when you spread it out it loses its continuity and you can travel through time almost the same way you travel through space. Sam provides me with the protection I need from the big theropods and from pteranodons. The North American Paleontological Society, which is the outfit I work for, has other similar vehicles for the Age of Reptiles, and it also has some for the Age of Mammals. But what you see when you look at Sam isn't exactly what you think you see. He doesn't really have a tail, and he has treads instead of legs. But an illusion field gives the impression of legs, stationary when he's stopped and moving when the treads are turning. And it makes you think he's got a great big tail."

"Gosh!" Skip said.

It was clear that he believed every word Carpenter had said, even the ones his hearrings could not possibly have coped with. Whether or not Princess Deidre did, it was impossible to tell.

"Well," Skip said, "it's all settled then. We're from Mars-present and you're from Earth-future. I knew you couldn't possibly be a Martian."

"One small question, Skip. Living on Mars, you can't possibly be used to Earth gravity, so how could you and your sister have climbed that tree?"

"We just climbed it is all. We didn't know there was any difference in gravity."

"But there is. Mars' gravity is only thirty-eight percent that of Earth's."

"You're talking about Mars-future, Mr. Carpenter. We're from Mars-present. Maybe gravity on Mars is stronger now than it will be in the future."

"That doesn't make any sense."

"Then maybe there's more gravity on Mars-future than you think. Have you ever been there, Mr. Carpenter? Has anyone from Earth-future?"

"No. But we know what the gravity is."

"Maybe if someone from Earth landed there and walked around, they'd be surprised."

Carpenter, realizing he was getting nowhere, relinquished the argument.

Perhaps the two kids really were from Mars. Perhaps they really had been kidnapped.

But they could be from Earth-future and still have been kidnapped.

He began to feel foolish about telling them about the Llonka time machine and about NAPS and about Sam. Probably they had learned all about modern-day paleontological work in school.

Then why had their eyes grown so large?

The sun was halfway down the afternoon slope of the Cretaceous sky, and its light, slightly muted by the hazy atmosphere, lay softly upon Deidre's and Skip's faces. He saw how thin their cheeks were; he looked at their thin arms. If they really had been kidnapped, the kidnappers certainly had not fed them very well.

Could they possibly be from Mars?

Granted, they did not look like Martians, but such an observation was absurd in view of the fact that he did not know what Martians were supposed to look like.

He thought of *Mariner 9* and *Vikings 1* and *2* and the two *Viking* Landers. Discounting the tetrahedral pyramids in Elysium, which looked like artifacts, the orbiters had photographed no hint of intelligent life whatsoever, and the landers had failed to come up with viable evidence of organic molecules. But neither the orbiters nor the landers had proved there was no life on Mars, and they definitely had not proved there might not have been long ago.

And then there were the hearrings. On his right index finger Carpenter wore a liaison ring which, to the unpracticed eye, looked like a cheap piece of jewelry he might have picked up in a discount store. It was encircled by a series of tiny, palpable nodules, each different to the touch, which gave him remote control of Sam. It was a device such as only an advanced technology could have produced; nevertheless, the technology that had created it was not advanced enough to have created two tiny ear pieces that influenced the auditory nerves.

But maybe the hearrings were something the *kids* had picked up in a discount store. Mentally he shook his head. Skip's lip movements had proved the language he spoke was not truly English despite the fact that the words Carpenter had been hearing *were* English.

He still was not convinced the kids were Martians, but whether they were or not, they had become his responsibility. And here they were, standing out in the open as though Cretaceous-16 were Central Park, the imminent prey of the first hungry theropod that happened along! "Okay, you two—get inside Sam where you'll be safe!"

He led the way over to the triceratank and climbed up into the driver's compartment. He did not bother to lower the nylon boarding ladder, but reached down instead and seized Deidre's hands and pulled her up beside him. Behind the seat was a sizable cabin—divided from the engine and battery compartment by a firewall—that contained a narrow built-in bunk, a little bolted-down table, two bolted-down chairs, a built-in cupboard, a built-in refrigerator, a sink, and a small electric stove. "Back there," he said, pointing.

Deidre was sliding around the seat's edge when a weird whistling came from above. She looked up through the windshield, and her face became as white as it had been when Carpenter first saw her in the ginkgo tree. "It's them!" she gasped. "They've found us!"

Following her gaze, Carpenter saw three huge winged shapes in the afternoon sky. Pteranodons! he thought. They were homing in on the triceratank like a trio of prehistoric dive bombers. Seizing Skip's hands, he pulled the boy up into the compartment and told him to get back into the cabin with his sister. He looked at the pteranodons again. They were too close for him to use Sam's howitzers. He slammed the passenger-side door and slid over behind the wheel.

The pteranodons meant business. The first one came so close its right aileron brushed Sam's frilled headshield, the fuselage of the second almost touched his back. The third made a shallower dive, then zoomed back into the sky with the others. Their tailjets left three twin wakes of smoke.

Chapter
2

CARPENTER SAT UP straight in the driver's seat. Ailerons? Fuselage? Tailjets?

Pteranodons?

He activated Sam's shield field and extended its invisible barrier to a distance of three feet beyond the reptivehicle's exterior. Then he threw the big machine into gear and directed it toward a nearby stand of trees. The pteranodons were now circling high overhead.

"Skip?"

"Yes, Mr. Carpenter?"

"When your sister saw the pteranodons, she said 'They've found us!' Who did she mean by 'they?'"

"I don't know what you mean by pteranodons, Mr. Carpenter, but I guess you must be referring to those three aircraft. We call them flyabouts. Three of the kidnappers are piloting them, and they're who Deidre meant by 'they.'"

"I see."

The plain was conducive to Sam's rapid progress, smooth, with only occasional hollows. Grass had yet to come fully into its own, and the ground cover consisted primarily of sassafras and laurel and dwarf magnolia. The magnolias were in bloom, and Carpenter, although he tried to steer Sam around them, was not always successful. At intervals flurries of blossoms rained like pink snowflakes on the windshield. Little lizards— blue ones, green ones, yellow ones—kept streaking from the reptivehicle's path.

Presently Sam reached the stand of trees and entered their fastness. Carpenter slowed him to a snail's pace. The trees were willows, and their foliage hid the sky. "These kidnappers you mentioned, Skip. I suppose they're from Mars too."

"Of course. Where else could they be from?" Skip's voice was more relaxed than before. "They abducted us from the Palace playground after disarming the guards. There are four of them—three men and a woman. They brought us here to their hideout in Eridahn for safekeeping. There's a fifth one who remained on Mars and who's going to collect the ransom. But the ransom is only part of their demands. They've ordered the Kingdom to start handing out food to the poor people. There aren't any real poor people, but the kidnappers hate the Establishment and want to be mean."

"Eridahn" had come through Carpenter's hearrings unscathed. "Is 'Eridahn' what you call Earth?"

"No. Just this small part of it. Greater Mars staked a claim with the idea of establishing a colony. The name Eridahn came into being all by itself because of all the wild animals."

"Zooland." Carpenter couldn't have thought of a better name himself. On the other hand, "Zooland" would have fit most of the whole planet at this stage of its history. "How big is the claim?"

"The white cliffs are the northern boundary. To the west it extends to the highlands and the mountains. To the south it extends to a big river, and on the east to the big sea. Between us and the sea is the city of Rimmon. Nobody lives there now except the kidnappers."

"There's a *city*? *Here*?"

"Yes. It was built almost fifty years ago. The—"

"Fifty of my years?"

"Yes, sir. The hearrings are pretty accurate with respect to translating time differences. The builders were going to build another city, but before they got started on it our geologists discovered that Earth wasn't nearly as stable as they'd thought and that a tectonic revolution—the same one you told Deidre and me about—was in progress, so the second city wasn't built. Then other things started to go wrong. The colonists who'd settled in the city had planted crops, but everything that grew was eaten up by herds of dinosaurs like the one that chased Deidre and me up the tree, and by herds of others that looked like Sam. Then big birds with leathery wings began attacking people in the city. And the sea! The colonists were going to fish there, but when they found out what kind of awful monsters it contained they wouldn't go near it any more. So when it was decided by the Greater Mars Parliament that it would be best if they came home, they couldn't wait to get into the ships the government sent for them."

"And now the city is the kidnappers' hideout?"

"It probably has been for years. The ship they brought us in is about a mile south of the city. Its top is camouflaged so that the Space Navy won't spot it if they should happen to get the idea Deidre and I are here and send a ship to Earth. But the Space Navy's too dumb to think of anything like that. The kidnappers didn't think Deidre and I would dare leave the city because of all the big reptiles, so they didn't guard us very close. About all we had to do was open the gate and walk out. We tried to find their ship so we could radio the Space Navy, but we got lost. Well, no, we didn't really get lost, a big long reptile came out of the swamps and chased us, and we got scared and ran for the plain. We must have walked on the plain for a long, long time, then that big animal with the funny mouth saw us and we climbed into the tree. That—that was when you came along, Mr. Carpenter."

Carpenter decided not to ask any more questions, at least for the time being. It seemed that every time he asked one it became more difficult for him to believe the kids were not from Mars.

The basis of his disbelief lay in the fact that they were so much like American children they could have passed for his son and daughter.

After all, the city—if there really was one—could be a terrestrial city, and both the kidnappers and the kids could have come from twentieth-century United States. NAPS did not have exclusive priority on time travel, and although Llonka time machines were not available to the public, one could have been stolen.

But if one had been, surely he would have heard about it.

And then there were the hearrings to contend with. They definitely suggested an alien technology and brought up another consideration as well, for if they were rendering an idiomatic translation of everything the boy said, he was bound to seem more than ever like an American simply because he talked like one.

But at the moment Skip's and his sister's provenance was not Carpenter's major concern. Whether they were from Mars or not, both they and he were being pursued by three clowns in three pseudopteranodons, and somehow he was going to have to give the pursuers the slip.

He had been guiding Sam on an erratic course through the stand of trees, and the reptivehicle had by now reached the stand's northern edge. Carpenter halted the big machine just within the outermost trees and studied the section of the plain beyond them. About a quarter of a mile away was another stand of trees, a much larger one. He looked at the sky. He saw no sign of the pteranodons. He listened, heard only the rhythmic purring of Sam's engine. But the pteranodons were not audible when they remained high above the ground, and the over-hanging foliage hid most of the sky.

There were four courses of action open to him: (1) he could keep Sam under cover until night; (2) he could alter the reptivehicle's illusion field so that Sam would blend in with the plain cover; (3) he could jump the reptivehicle back in time; (4) he could rev up its engine and make a dash for the stand of trees.

He decided on number 4. "Hold on, you guys," he said, and gunned Sam out of the woods.

SKRRRREEEEEEEEEEEEEK! one of the pteranodons went as it nearly sideswiped the shield field.

Carpenter watched it wobble. Before it straightened out and shot back into the sky, he saw a bearded face in its forward floor-viewport and realized the pilot was lying in a prone position between the long, flat wings. He also detected a bomb carrier on the vehicle's belly and spotted three small egg-shaped bombs.

All was not lost. He could still alter Sam's illusion field, and he could still jump the reptivehicle back in time. But to follow either course while Sam was out in the open would betray a trump card, and there was no real need to, for if worse came to worse he could blast the pteranodons from the sky with charges from Sam's horn-howitzers. So he let Sam continue his rush toward the trees.

A toppled magnolia enveloped the triceratank in an evanescent squall of pink snowflakes. In the distance to his right, Carpenter saw a herd of ceratopsians. Sam's sentient brethren. The springtime sky was deep blue. The pteranodons were circling like black Messerschmitts.

Skip climbed over the back of the driver's seat and sat down close to Carpenter. He saw that the boy was trembling. Glancing over his shoulder, he saw that Deidre's face was pale. "Hey, you guys—what're you worried about? Sam'll protect you."

"We're—we're not afraid that the kidnappers'll kill us," Skip said. "We're just afraid they may get us back. They won't kill us yet because they may have to radio our voices to Greater Mars again in case the ransom doesn't come through and their other demands aren't met."

"Their bombs won't bother us as long as Sam's shield field is on."

"No, but they can drop one ahead of us and—"

It was as though one of the pilots heard what Skip said, for a laurel directly in Sam's path was transformed into a flurry of leaves and shattered limbs, and a crater appeared where it had stood. There was a muffled *bang*!

Carpenter managed to avoid the crater, although Sam wobbled for a moment. Fortunately the woods were close, and a few seconds later Carpenter guided Sam into them. They consisted of a mixture of ginkgoes and willows, more thinly scattered than the trees in the previous stand.

He slowed Sam to a walk. "I'll tell you what, Skip. Why don't you go back in the cabin with your sister and the two of you get yourselves something to eat. I don't know what kind of food you're accustomed to, but Sam is stocked with just about everything you can think of. For starters, you'll find some square vacuum containers in the cupboard—they contain sandwiches. Just pull the little tab on top to open them. And in the refrigerator you'll find some tall bottles with circles of little stars around their necks—they contain pop, which is a sweet, flavored soda water. Just twist the cap at the top counterclockwise—to the left. Dig in."

He determined Sam's course through the woods by using the thickness of the foliage as an index. Occasionally he caught glimpses of his pursuers through interstices, but he was certain the pilots could not see the reptivehicle. Maybe he should park it under the trees and remain in the woods all night. This would give him time to decide what he should do about the kids. To figure out whether they were truly Martians or whether he was on the receiving end of an elaborate con job.

Skip handed him a ham sandwich over the back of the driver's seat. "Deidre sent you up a sandwich, Mr. Carpenter."

"I did not!"

"You did so! You handed it to me and pointed to him."

"I wasn't pointing at him!"

"You were so!"

"Why don't you hand me up a bottle of pop too, Princess," Carpenter said. "Root beer. You can tell it's root beer by the brown color."

There was a long silence. Then, above the purring of Sam's engine, he heard the refrigerator door open and close and then the *pop*! of a cap being removed. Then a small hand appeared holding a bottle of root beer. "Thank you, Princess."

"Can I sit up front?" Skip asked.

"Sure."

The boy clambered over the top of the seat. "Deidre would like to sit up front too," he whispered into Carpenter's ear.

"Tell her okay," Carpenter whispered back.

"Come on up, Deidre."

Sam's head was better than five feet wide, but the driver's seat was only four. Still, there was plenty of room when Deidre slid down on the other side of Skip. Both were eating sandwiches and drinking pop. Carpenter wondered how many sandwiches they had eaten already. It did not matter. They were more than welcome to all they wanted. There was enough food in Sam's larder to last two grown men two weeks.

He could see Deidre's face sideways and the back of her head when she looked out Sam's right lateral window. Not once did she look in his direction. Well, after all, he could hardly expect her to. He was only a truck driver and she was a princess. NAPS classified him as a past holographer and paid him handsomely, but about all he ever had to do was drive reptivehicles and mammalmobiles. Trucks.

Despite Deidre's aloofness, he began to feel like an indulgent parent taking his kids on an excursion through a zoo. And such a zoo! Lizards were everywhere, and they were almost every color under the sun. An ankylosaur watched Sam's passage from behind a large clump of sedges, but the big armored dinosaur did not argue Sam's right of way. An ornithomime was scared half out of its wits by the reptivehicle's approach and brought to mind an ostrich as it hid itself behind a tree. Two anatosaurs—full-grown ones—who were lunching on leaves decided to lunch somewhere else. A struthiomime—a toothless dinosaur even more ostrichlike then *Ornithomimus*—hightailed it across a glade. There were snakes and turtles as well as lizards, and in the trees were strange birds with teeth.

Carpenter, thinking of *Tyrannosaurus rex*, kept his eye peeled in case one of the giant theropods might be out for a stroll.

Abruptly there was an explosion in Sam's path, and a crater appeared. Clods of dirt rained down on the windshield. "They've spotted us!" Skip cried.

Carpenter avoided the crater and plunged Sam into a thicker part of the woods. He was driving with one hand, holding his ham sandwich in the other, the bottle of root beer braced between his legs. Hurriedly he finished the sandwich and tossed off the rest of the pop and set the bottle on the floor. Slowing Sam to a crawl, he glanced at his wristwatch: 5:46 P.M. It would not be dark for a long time. He glanced at the kids. They had forgotten their sandwiches and pop and were staring up through Sam's curved windshield at the little patches of sky that showed through the foliage. "I think it's high time we gave them the slip, don't you?"

"But how can we, Mr. Carpenter?" Skip asked. "They can spot us through the trees, and if we go out on the plain they'll ring Sam with craters and force you to give Deidre and me back to them."

"I think you've forgotten the most important thing I told you about Sam. He can jump back in time."

Skip's apprehension vanished, and Deidre actually looked at Carpenter. Carpenter grinned. "Come on, you two—finish your sandwiches and stop worrying."

Deidre whispered something into Skip's ear, then Skip said, "Deidre says to jump back five days. That way they'll never find us because they won't be here yet."

"And you two wouldn't be either. We'd sort of drive Time up a tree. Time plays along with minor paradoxes, but if we were to give it one like that it might cancel you kids from the scroll, and me too, since I wouldn't be here yet either. Also," Carpenter continued, "jumpbacks require a lot of power, and if a part-time time machine like Sam were to jump back much more than four days, he'd burn his batteries out. So what I think we'd better do is settle for an hour."

The calculations involved in jumpbacks increased as the temporal distance decreased. Carpenter put Sam on autopilot and turned on the reptivehicle's terrainometer. The woods remained thick, and there was no danger at the moment of being spotted by the kidnappers. He began punching out arithmetical brain-twisters on the compact Llonka computer which was built into the control panel.

Skip leaned forward to obtain a better view of the computation screen. "Your numerals are almost like ours, Mr. Carpenter," he said, reading the figures that had appeared. "If it'll help matters, Deidre can compute multiplications like that in her head. Deidre, how much is 828,464,280 times 4,692,438,921?"

"3,887,518,032,130,241,880," Deidre answered.

"I think I'd better check it out to make sure," Carpenter said drily. He touched a small button, and the figures 3,887,518,032,130,241,880 appeared on the screen. He stared at them.

"She's a mathematical genius," Skip said. "I'm a mechanical genius myself. The members of the Royal Scientific Academy say its unusual for a prince and a princess to be geniuses. They say that usually the members of the Royal Family are dumbbells, although of course they don't use that word. I'll bet they're having a fit that we were kidnapped."

"I imagine your parents are having an even bigger fit."

"Well, kind of. If they don't get Deidre and me back they'll have to dig up a new successor somewhere, and that means bringing one of our cousins into the realm, and they won't like that at all."

"I don't mean having a fit about having to find a new successor. I mean having a fit about you kids being in danger."

"I don't think they're much concerned about that. We're kind of strangers to them. We don't even live in the same part of the palace they do, and about the only time they see us is during public appearances and during royal weddings when the whole family has to be present."

"Listen," Carpenter said, "the tale you've told me is already tall enough, so don't make it any taller. Almost everybody cares about their kids, even kings and queens."

"Maybe in Earth-future, but not in Mars-present. In Mars-present no one cares about their kids. I guess it sounds strange to you because I haven't told you about desentimentalization. You see, everybody in Greater Mars is desentimentalized at the age of thirteen. It's a simple brain operation that almost any surgeon can perform. It was discovered long ago that sentiment is the basic instability factor, and that without refined and tender emotions—like love and affection and compassion—tripping people up all the time, civilization can stay on a much more even keel. Once a person is desentimentalized he becomes capable of making calm, cool decisions that are always in keeping with pure logic. Hatred still trips people up once in a while, but as a rule when they're desentimentalized they attain maximum efficiency and can see the logical course to follow in order to get ahead in life and make lots of money. Of course Deidre's and my parents don't have to think about getting ahead and making money, but they have the same objective outlook on life all the other Greater Martians do. So you see, they just can't care much about Deidre and me. They're concerned about our absence, sure, but it's impossible for them to be emotionally concerned about us."

Carpenter regarded Skip's solemn face and Deidre's solemn profile. "Yes, I guess I do see at that."

"The state itself is probably more concerned about our abduction than our parents are. In Greater Mars it's traditional to have a king or a queen and a prince or a princess to succeed whoever's on the throne. Not because the king or the queen has much to do with the function of government but because they're there. Early in our history the king or the queen ruled with an iron hand. Now the people rule themselves, or think they do, but since there's always been a Royal Family they simply have to have one to look up to."

"We have a government like that on Earth, but its people aren't desentimentalized."

"You can be desentimentalized and still need a Royal Family. A Royal Family represents money and position and functions as a sort of ideal."

At this point Carpenter realized that he'd been talking and listening to the boy as though he and his sister really were from Mars. It dawned on him that his doubts had vanished and that he now believed everything the boy had told him. Skip's clear blue eyes had said all along that he was telling the truth, and Carpenter should have believed him in the first place, but his common sense had gotten in the way.

Sometimes, he reflected, a man's common sense could be his worst enemy. Ptolemy had used his common sense when he put together his absurd universe. Medieval doctors had used their common sense when they bled their patients. Columbus had used his common sense when he called the inhabitants of Watling Island Indians.

So the kids were from Mars and they'd been kidnapped and had got away, and they were a princess and a prince. He would take it from there. He finished his computations, threw the jumpback switch, and said, "Here we go, you guys!" There was a brief shimmering effect both inside and outside the triceratank and an almost imperceptible jar. So smoothly did the transition take place that Sam did not lose a step in his self-propelled walk.

_____Chapter

_____3

CARPENTER SET HIS watch back from 5:54 P.M. to 4:54 P.M., deactivated the terrainometer, and took over manual control of Sam. Sam's control board clock had reset itself. When the woods ended, Carpenter drove the reptivehicle out into the sunlight. "Take a look at the sky, kids. See any so-called pteranodons?"

They peered up through the windshield. Skip leaned forward so he could see back over the woods. "Not a one, Mr. Carpenter."

Carpenter gunned Sam. "We'd better be long gone before they get here. And we'd better not leave any visible tracks."

There had been no recent rainfall and the ground was hard. He followed an erratic route, meticulously avoiding growths that would have been crushed beneath Sam's treads and circumventing places where nothing grew at all. In most cases the plain cover was resilient enough to spring back into shape after the reptivehicle passed over it. When they came to a creek, he drove Sam up its bed for about a mile.

Deidre whispered something into Skip's ear, and Skip said, "Deidre wants to know how far Sam could jump into the future if his diffusion unit didn't have a governor."

"Probably no farther than he can jump into the past. At the very most, four and a half days. Any farther and his batteries would probably burn out. But if I were to drive him into the photon field of my entry point and the big Llonka machine in NAPS' laboratory took over, his range would be 74,051,622 years, three and a half months, plus the seven or eight hours I've been here. But that's my present, so it isn't really the future for me at all, although it certainly would be for you kids. Genuine future travel is forbidden because of the possible complications that could arise from it and because people are generally better off if they don't know what's going to happen tomorrow."

There was a silence. Then: "What's Mars like in your time?" Skip asked.

Carpenter decided to lie a little. "We don't really know very much about it because we don't have manned interplanetary travel."

"I'll bet it's a lot different than it is today."

"Well, after all," Carpenter said, "74,051,622 years." It was time to change the subject. "You mentioned a Space Navy. Is there any chance of their finding out that the kidnappers brought you here?"

"No. They're not very smart, Mr. Carpenter."

"If they did find out, how long would it take them to get here?"

"Right now, Earth and Mars are in opposition—about fifty million miles apart. The Space Navy could make the trip in a little less than five days."

"But that's impossible!" Carpenter objected.

"Not for a big, fast Martian ship. Greater Mars specializes in space travel. Our ships use an antimass reactor for take-off, then they switch over to cation drive. They can build up pretty high velocities. If it weren't for having to begin decelerating midway between the two planets, they could make the journey

in next to no time at all. Don't you have *any* interplanetary
ships at all, Mr. Carpenter?"

"We got to the moon," Carpenter said, "but you can hardly
call that an interplanetary voyage."

And the moon, he reflected, is just about as far as we're
going to get. For since the invention of the Llonka time machine, monies that otherwise might have gone into space exploration had gone and were going into the exploration of the
past.

Sam was now heading in a northerly direction, and the cliffs,
although still several miles away, were clearly visible between
the scattered stands of trees. Carpenter wondered if he should
reverse the triceratank's direction and head for the river and
the photon field, and take the kids to A.D. 1998. But if he went
back the way they'd come, he'd run the risk of Sam's being
spotted, and in any case he wasn't at all certain that he should
take the kids to the twentieth century. They might look like
modern American children, and certainly Skip seemed to talk
like one, thanks to the hearrings in Carpenter's ears, but modern
American children they were not. They were Martians, and as
though further to compound the problem, they were a princess
and a prince.

Undoubtedly they were versatile, but even so, they could
hardly be expected to accept with equanimity the values, or
lack thereof, of twentieth-century Western Civilization. And
what would he do with them if he did take them to A.D. 1998?
Farm them out for adoption? Adopt them himself? He smiled
ruefully. How could he adopt two children when the only home
he had was a hotel room?

He could buy a real home, of course.

But even assuming he did adopt them, there were other
considerations. How in the world could he send a princess
capable of multiplying 828,464,280 times 4,692,438,921 in
her head and coming up with the right answer to public, or
even private, school? A princess moreover who wouldn't even
talk to anyone unless the person was a member of Martian
royalty? He could just see her walking down a school corridor,
her nose high in the air, and the other kids making fun of her
and calling her Stuck-up and other mean names, and hating

her not only because she was conceited but because she was three times as smart as they were.

Skip, no doubt, would fare better, but he would have a hard time too.

One possible way out of the dilemma would be to take them to A.D. 1998, keep them there for a week or two, and then take them back to Eridahn on the chance that the Space Navy would have traced the kidnappers by then and have apprehended them and have launched a search for the two children. But according to Skip, the Space Navy wasn't smart enough to trace the kidnappers, and the plan had an even more vehement drawback: NAPS. A round-time-trip of 74,051,622 years cost a fortune. The holograms Sam had taken would partially justify Carpenter's return from this one sans knowledge of the origin of the fossil, but if he were to ask NAPS if he could make another such trip just to take the kids back, the wrath of the Society would become as the whirlwind that had assailed Job. He could argue till he was blue in the face that the kids were Martians and that the kidnappers who had brought them to Earth might be tied in with the origin of the fossil, but NAPS wouldn't believe him any more than he'd at first believed Skip.

He looked at his watch: 5:21. If he headed for the field, night would fall before he got there, and he didn't care to drive in the dark. Whatever he did about the kids would have to wait till tomorrow. He looked at the cliffs. They were quite close now. "How'd you guys like to camp out?"

Skip looked at him. So did Deidre. "Camp out?" Skip asked.

"Sure. We'll build a fire, cook our food over it, spread out blankets on the ground—regular American-Indian style."

"What's American-Indian style?"

He told them about the Arapahoes and the Cheyennes and the Crows and the Apaches, and about the buffalo and the Great Plains and Custer's last stand and about Geronimo and Sitting Bull and Cochise, and then he told them about the Indians of the east, about Deganawida and Hiawatha founding the League of Five Nations and about Handsome Lake and the Four Messengers, and about the Cherokees and the Trail of Tears, and all the while he talked their eyes remained fixed on his face as though it were the sun coming up in the morning after a long, cold night. Or at least this was so till Princess

Deidre caught him looking at her; she then wiped the fascination from her face and put her princess look back on.

The cliffs rose ever higher into the sky, whiter than ever in the slanted rays of the sun. Although from a distance they looked like chalk, they were limestone. Beyond a frieze of ginkgoes he found a large concavity at their base and parked Sam well within it. He then extended the shield field into a semihemisphere that enclosed the concavity and a sizable area of ground before it, and extended the illusion field into a semi-hemisphere just within the shield field, adjusting the former's color scheme to conform to the whiteness of the cliffs. Seen from without, the area now should appear as a large bulge at the cliffs' base, but since the illusion field was one way, Carpenter and the kids were able to see through the walls of their sanctum sanctorum.

Sam had lost his identity. He was now a large tank with a big frilled head.

After checking the area for reptiles and finding only a few small lizards, Carpenter put Skip and Deidre to work gathering firewood. Or, rather, he put Skip to work. Deidre would have no part of such demeaning labor and stood to one side disdainfully watching her brother. Skip brought to mind a Boy Scout bucking for a merit badge. There was a plenitude of firewood available in the form of dead ginkgo branches, and soon he had built a sizable pile. By this time he had lost what little reserve he had left and cried, "Can I help build the fire, Mr. Carpenter? Can I? Can I? Can I?"

"I don't see why not," Carpenter said.

By now night had fallen. The walls of the cliff turned rosy, then lightened to pale yellow as the young flames of the campfire grew into mature ones. After the kids washed up in Sam's sink, Carpenter found two new combs on the topmost cupboard shelf where the toilet articles were stored and handed one to each of them. He washed up himself, then began digging among the provisions for fare suitable for an outdoor cookout. Miss Sands was an imaginative provisioner, and he was not particularly surprised to find several dozen wieners in the refrigerator and four packages of wiener rolls in the cupboard. He also found mustard and relish. He grabbed a table knife and carried the rolls, wieners, mustard, and relish outside and placed them on a flat rock near the fire. Then he found a yard-long stick, sharpened one end of it with his pocketknife, and showed Skip how to impale a wiener on the sharpened end and how to roast it over the flames. When the wiener split, he showed the boy how to place it on an open roll and how to spread mustard and relish over it. "Do you think your sister is hungry?"

"I don't know," Skip said, taking a big bite of the hot dog. He chewed and swallowed it. "Boy!"

"Do you think if I fixed her a hot dog she'd eat it?"

"She might."

Carpenter found and sharpened another stick, impaled a wiener on the sharpened end, and held it over the flames. Skip, having dispatched his first hot dog, began preparing another. Deidre, standing a little to one side, watched the proceedings with a mixture of scorn and curiosity, curiosity predominating. Her autumn-aster eyes seemed to have grown larger. She did not look much like a princess in her disheveled and dirty pantaloons and blouse, although her hair was now neatly combed. Even in the firelight, its hue was that of buttercups. When the wiener split, Carpenter placed it on a roll and layered it with mustard and relish. He offered it to her. "Try it and see if you like it, Pumpkin."

At first he didn't think she was going to take it. Then she held out her hand and he placed the hot dog in it. He turned back to the fire to fix one for himself. A few minutes later when he glanced at her, her hot dog was gone and she was whispering to Skip.

"Oh, all right!" Skip said. After finding another stick, he borrowed Carpenter's pocketknife and sharpened it. He speared a wiener with it, speared one with his own stick, and held both wieners over the flames. When they split, he put them on rolls, and both kids layered the hot dogs with mustard and relish. Deidre took a big bite of hers, and Carpenter turned away so she would not see him smiling.

He sharpened another stick for himself, and after roasting and eating two hot dogs, he headed for Sam's cabin. He had already lowered the nylon boarding ladder so the kids could climb in and out. In the cabin, he made cocoa on Sam's stove. Somehow the campout did not seem quite complete. Was it conceivable, he wondered, that Miss Sands, in including wieners and rolls and mustard and relish among the provisions, had also included marshmallows? He went through the cupboard. Sure enough, there was a big bag of them. Triumphantly he carried it outside, along with the pot of cocoa and three cups. After pouring the cocoa, he opened the bag. "You kids haven't seen anything yet."

Before their wondering eyes he stuck a marshmallow on the end of his stick and held it over the diminishing flames. The kids stared. The marshmallow turned golden brown. He took it off the stick and took a small bite of it. "Not bad," he said.

Skip already had one on his own stick and now he held it over the flames. Deidre had moved closer to the fire, her eyes locked on the marshmallow. It had already turned golden brown. Skip, unable to wait any longer, removed it from the stick and tasted it. "Wow!"

Without saying anything, Carpenter picked up the stick Skip had sharpened for Deidre, stuck one of the marshmallows on it, and handed the stick to her. A second later she was standing beside Skip, who was roasting his second one, both marshmallows turning golden brown over the flames.

There weren't many left when at last the flames receded into glowing embers. "You kids ever slept outside before?" Carpenter asked.

Skip shook his head. "Of course, you could sleep in Sam," Carpenter said. "One of you could sleep in the bunk and I could make a blanket bed for the other on the floor and—"

"No, we'd rather sleep outside," Skip said. "Like the Indians. Wouldn't we, Deidre?"

Deidre nodded.

There was still enough light coming from the fire to see by, so there was no need to turn on the big searchlight which was built into Sam's steel head-shield. Carpenter set about collecting fallen ginkgo branches that were still resilient and aligned them into makeshift mattresses. Then he opened Sam's storage compartment, which was located beneath the cabin floor. It contained enough blankets to accommodate a small army. He lugged a big armful over to the makeshift mattresses and covered each with three blankets. After returning to the compartment for more, he folded two into makeshift pillows and spread one on each bed so the kids would be able to cover themselves.

It was warm now, but the shield field, while impervious to dinosaurs, was not impervious to the night air, and the temperature would drop toward dawn.

Deidre's and Skip's faces betrayed their tiredness, but Skip lingered when Carpenter said it was time to call it a day. Deidre, without a word, chose one of the bough beds, took off her boots, lay down, and covered herself up to her chin. Skip watched Carpenter prepare his bed, and when Carpenter sat down on it, the boy sat down beside him. "Hey," Carpenter said, "this is my bed."

"I know. I'm—I'm not really tired yet."

"You look like you're tired."

"I'm not, though."

All evening long, grunts and growls and groans had been coming from beyond the shield field; now, all of a sudden, they were superseded by an awesome noise that brought to Carpenter's mind a road-repair machine breaking up old pavement. The ground trembled, and the few tiny flames that still lingered among the embers of the campfire flickered wildly.

"Sounds like old *Tyrannosaurus* himself," Carpenter said. "Probably out looking for a snack in the form of an ornithomime or two."

"Tyrannosaurus?"

Carpenter described the giant tyrannosaur. He had never seen one in the flesh, but on previous pasttrips he had met its predecessors, *Allosaurus* and *Gorgosaurus*. When he finished, Skip nodded. "He's another of the reasons the colonists were in such a hurry to leave. Gosh, you sure have some terrible monsters here on Earth, Mr. Carpenter!"

"We don't have them in my time. They'll only be around for a few more million years. Once there must have been similar creatures on Mars."

"No. There were never any."

"But there must have been some form of prehominid life."

Skip shook his head. "No. If there was, our paleontologists would have discovered some sign of it. The only life there's ever been on Mars is the same kind of life that's there now, and even that kind has only been on the planet since the last ice age. Are all the dinosaurs going to die out, Mr. Carpenter?"

"All the big ones."

"What's going to happen to them?"

"Nobody in my time knows what happened to them. When the Cretaceous Period ended, they disappeared—Cretaceous is what we call this particular time phase. The North American Paleontological Society thought they were going to find out what happened when they began using Llonka time machines, but they've never been able to. Whenever I or one of the other past holographers aims for the last thousand years or so of the Cretaceous, we wind up in a place–time much farther back than the one we wanted."

"The Ku, I'll bet. They don't want you to find out."

Like Eridahn, the word had come through Carpenter's hearrings unscathed. "The Ku?"

"They seeded Mars. With human and other forms of life. It must be that someday they're going to seed Earth with human life too. Human life exactly like the human life on Mars. Your having come back here from the future proves it."

"If they're going to seed Earth with human life, why did they seed it first with reptiles?"

"The reptiles are probably an experiment. One that maybe didn't work."

Carpenter thought of Darwin, but he saw no point in outlining the theory of evolution for the benefit of a nine-year-old boy from Mars. "What exactly are the Ku, Skip?"

"Nobody knows. It's theorized they're from another galaxy. But nobody knows why they do things. The colonists who lived here claimed they saw them."

"Here? On Earth?"

"Yes. And people on Mars claim they've seen them too. And the Ku have left evidence of themselves."

"What kind of evidence?"

"Great big monuments."

"Do your *scientists* believe they seeded Mars?"

"They're positive."

At this point the "road-repair machine" struck a bad stretch of pavement and, judging from the ungodly series of sounds that ensued, blew a rod to boot. Skip moved closer to Carpenter. "Not to worry," Carpenter reassured him. "An army of tyrannosaurs couldn't break through that shield field."

"Are you married, Mr. Carpenter?"

The question was apropos of nothing, insofar as Carpenter could see. He had a hunch that Skip was trying to con him into talking so he could stay up longer. "I assume that by 'married' you mean a lifetime union of a man and a woman."

"Yes. A business-love relationship. On Mars the state sees to it that each member of the union is compatible with the other."

"How can two people tell whether they love each other when they're desentimentalized?"

"Well, they can't, really. That's why the state is so strict about the compatibility part. Are you married?" Skip asked again.

"No."

"Why not? You're old enough to be."

"Well, you see, in Earth-future it's sort of a different proposition from what you have in Mars-present. The state has nothing to do with the deal, and business doesn't play a part either, although maybe it should. What happens is, a man falls in love with a woman and she falls in love with him, and then in most cases they get married. Lots of times, though, the marriage turns out to be a mistake and doesn't work."

"I guess compatibility is pretty hard to come by if you're not desentimentalized."

"That would certainly seem to be our weak point."

"I should think that by now, with only love to go by, some girl would certainly have fallen in love with you, Mr. Carpenter, and you with her."

"Sometimes," Carpenter said, "a man falls in love with a girl and she doesn't fall in love back."

"Is that what happened to you, Mr. Carpenter?"

Deidre turned on her side beneath her blanket. Carpenter wondered if she was still awake. "Yes," he said, "that's what happened to me." He found himself telling Skip about Miss Sands. It seemed he had talked more tonight than he had for years, and that was probably true, because for years he really had not had anyone to talk to—anyone, that is, who would have been more than politely interested in what he had to say. "There's this girl named Miss Sands. She's the North American Paleontological Society's chronologist and pasttrip provisioner. Her first name is Elaine, but everybody calls her Sandy. Except me. I—I just call her Miss Sands. She sees to it that nobody forgets anything when he retrotravels and she pinpoints the place–time he's going to with the carbon-14 retroscope and then focuses the area with the timescope. Then she and her assistant, Peter Fields, remain on the alert, ready to come to the rescue if the holographer sends back a can of chicken soup. That's our distress signal. You see, in our language, sometimes the word chicken means fear."

"Are you in love with her, Mr. Carpenter?"

"I've been in love with her ever since I first saw her."

"What did she say when you told her?"

"I *didn't* tell her. I never dared. You see, she's not just an ordinary run-of-the-mill girl. She's something special. And I'm just one of the holographers she does time-work for, so maybe that's one of the reasons she's never seemed to notice me. Sometimes, though, I get the impression that to her I'm just a stick of wood. About the only conversations we ever have is when I say good morning to her and she says good morning back. Even then she won't even look at me. You see, with a girl like her you don't just barge right up and say 'I love you.' You sort of worship her from afar and wait for her to notice you're alive. I can just imagine what she'd say if I did tell her I loved her. I can just imagine!"

"Well, gosh," Skip said, "it wouldn't hurt to try it and see."

Carpenter shook his head. "I haven't got the nerve. Anyway, I've no right to expect her to love me back. All I am is a truck driver. What could I ever do for a girl like her?"

"You could love her. You see, Mr. Carpenter, I haven't been desentimentalized yet, so I know what real love is. And I should think that if you really loved a girl, she wouldn't have a right to expect much of anything else."

"It doesn't work that way. You people in Mars-present have the right idea. A marriage should be based on both love *and* business, even if the love isn't quite the real thing. You can love someone all you please, but unless the marriage has something else to hold it together, it won't work."

"I think this is a silly argument, Mr. Carpenter, because I'll bet truck drivers like you make lots of money."

"And *I* think," Carpenter said, "that it's high time a certain young man I know should go to bed."

"But I'm not tired."

"You're so tired you'll fall asleep the second you close your eyes."

Reluctantly Skip got to his feet. "What do people in Earth-future say when they go to bed?"

"They say good night. And in the morning when they get up and see someone, they say good morning."

"Good night, Mr. Carpenter."

"Good night, Skip."

Carpenter watched him walk over to his bough bed and remove his boots and slip beneath the topmost blanket. Presently his even breathing reached Carpenter's ears. Not long afterward Deidre's even breathing joined it. Yes, she had been awake.

Her blanket had slipped down from her shoulders. He went over and pulled it back up to her chin. She turned from one side to the other, and the glow from the campfire gave a reddish tint to her buttercup-color hair. He wondered if there were buttercup-pied meadows on Mars like the ones on 1998 Earth, and he thought there probably were, and he pictured the sun rising above the Martian horizon and ushering in a dew-jeweled day.

He was tired, but he did not think he could sleep. He walked over to the other side of the dying fire and stared out into the darkness beyond the shield field. The big theropod had departed, and the lesser Cretaceous creatures were making their presence known. He glimpsed the ostrich-shapes of several struthiomimes and saw the big blur of an ankylosaur near the frieze of ginkgo trees. He heard the scurryings of insectivores. A moon subtly different from the one he was accustomed to hovered high in the sky. It was a gibbous moon. No doubt the difference arose from the lesser number of craters marring its face.

He realized presently that although he was still looking at the moon he was no longer seeing it. Instead he was seeing the campfire, the campfire as it had been a short time ago, with the girl and the boy roasting marshmallows over its fading flames. Why had he not gotten married and had children? he wondered suddenly. Plenty of pretty girls had looked his way. Why had he passed them up, only to fall hopelessly in love at the age of thirty-two with a girl who preferred not to know he was alive? What ever had given him the notion that the independence of celibacy was somehow superior to the contentment derived from loving and being loved? That a lonely room in a hotel constituted a man's castle and that drinks drunk in dimlit bars with sleazy women whose faces he could not remember the next day were all a man needed to sustain him after a day's or a week's work was done?

He had pursued so many endeavors. At one time he had been an amateur boxer, at a later time, a lumberjack. Then he had climbed mountains in Tibet. Not Everest, but some almost as big. For several years he had been a merchant seaman, and after that, a steelworker. Finally he had wound up as a holographer of pasttimes.

There had been two glasses, one full, one empty. He had chosen the empty one.

And yet it had not proved to be empty after all, for he had found in the past a treasure that in the future he had thrown away. The treasure of a girl and a boy.

The night had grown chill. He went over to Sam and climbed into the driver's compartment and removed a small raze pistol from its holster in the driver's side door and slipped it into his belt. Back outside he added wood to the dying fire, then removed his boots and lay down on his bough bed. He laid the pistol on the ground within easy reach, although he was certain he would have no need for it, then he set his mental alarm to awake him at the first sign of day. He was sure the kidnappers had not tracked Sam, but the false bulge the illusion field had brought into being at the cliffs' base would appear incongruous in broad daylight and if the kidnappers continued their search they might guess its true nature. It was imperative that he find a safer hiding place for the kids till he decided what to do with them.

He listened to the crackling of the reborn fire. He watched the pale flickerings the new flames cast upon the children's faces. A little lizard regarded him with golden eyes from a rock several feet away. In the distance a dinosaur went *waroompf!* Beside him in the Mesozoic night the two children breathed softly in their bough beds. At last he slept.

* * *

He awoke in dawnlight. The fire had gone out. He did not build a new one for it would take too much time. He carried the cocoa pot and the three cups into Sam's cabin, and, after cleaning up, washed them in Sam's sink. He set about fixing another potful. It would have to do for the morning meal. Later on, after he found a safer hiding place, he would fix a bounteous breakfast for the kids.

He poured a cup of cocoa for himself and left it in the cabin and took the pot and the two other cups outside. The kids were still sound asleep. "Wake up, you guys—it's time to get the show on the road."

The show did not get very far. In fact, it did not even reach the road. Carpenter made two mistakes. He returned his raze pistol to its holster in the driver's side door and, after retracting the illusion field and altering it so it would turn the reptivehicle back into a ceratopsian, he deactivated Sam's shield field to give the batteries a brief break. When, after drinking his cocoa, he jumped down from the driver's compartment to the ground, three figures emerged from behind the frieze of ginkgoes and spread out. One halted at ten o'clock, one at twelve, and one at two. Each was armed with a long silvery rifle, and the muzzle of each weapon was directed at Carpenter's chest.

_____**Chapter**

_____4

THE FIGURE AT twelve o'clock was that of a
woman. She was tall and lean, and had a hard, beautiful face.
Her black hair fell to her shoulders, and she had a vivid scar
on her right cheek. She appeared to be about Carpenter's age.

The figures at ten and two o'clock were those of men. They
too appeared to be about Carpenter's age. Both had hard, bearded
faces. The ten-o'clock figure was thin and wiry, the two-o'clock
one was tall—much taller than the woman. He had big teeth
that gave his face an apelike aspect. He was smiling.

Both men had long brown hair which needed combing. They
were wearing grimy coveralllike garments and dirty boots. The
woman was similarly clothed.

Carpenter palpated the liaison ring on his index finger with
his thumb. When he felt a tiny square nodule he depressed it,
and Sam, who was facing away from the cliffs, charged straight
for the plain, forcing the woman to jump out of his path. So

great was his velocity, his passenger-side door, which Carpenter had left open, slammed shut.

The woman and the thin, wiry man began shooting at the reptivehicle just before it disappeared beyond the ginkgoes. Their rifles emitted laserlike beams, but apparently none found their mark, for the purring of Sam's engine continued without interruption and gradually faded away as he moved farther out on the plain.

The autopilot, which the ring had activated and programmed, would keep Sam moving for five miles, and his terrainometer, which the ring had also activated, would keep him from blundering into gullies or bumping into trees.

The three kidnappers were furious. Particularly the tall one with the ape-teeth, who now advanced upon Carpenter. Deidre and Skip had been standing all this while like statues, their half-empty cocoa cups forgotten in their hands. Now Skip cried, "Watch out for him, Mr. Carpenter—he's mean!"

The bleakness of the tall man's face was apparent even through his beard. His blue eyes were squinted and were as bleak as his face. He halted a few feet from Carpenter. "So you had a buddy with you."

Carpenter nodded. It was fine with him if the kidnappers thought someone drove Sam off.

"What're you doing here? Where're you from?"

The tall man was not wearing hearrings, so Carpenter saw no point in answering. "He's from the future," Skip said. "He can't speak any of the Martian languages."

"You shut up!" the tall man snapped.

The other two kidnappers had now closed in. The woman said, "He knows where his buddy went. Make him tell us, Floyd."

The tall man dug the muzzle of his rifle into Carpenter's chest. "We don't like secrets. Where'd he go?"

"I told you," Skip cried, "he can't speak our language!"

The woman walked over to where Skip and Deidre were standing. "You tell us then," she said to Skip.

"I don't know."

The woman faced Deidre. "I'm sure the princess knows."

Deidre looked at the woman as though she were a worm that had just crawled out of a wormhole. Infuriated, the kidnapper screamed, "You tell me or I'll break your conceited little neck!"

Deidre spat in her face. The woman removed one hand from her rifle and aimed a blow at Deidre's face. Carpenter forgot both Floyd and the rifle, and started toward them. But Floyd did not forget him, and swung the butt of the rifle around in a vicious arc toward Carpenter's head. Carpenter, with a boxer's reflex, blocked the blow with his forearm, but it knocked him to the ground. A second later the rifle's muzzle was inches from his nose.

Deidre had dodged the woman's blow. Now the third kidnapper stepped forward. "A big machine like that'll leave a trail, Floyd. Let's follow it."

"It didn't leave one yesterday."

"We didn't know where to look for it is all. Come on, let's go."

The muzzle of the rifle moved an inch to the left of Carpenter's nose. Another inch. Then it moved away altogether. "Search him and tie him up," Floyd told the thin, wiry man.

Carpenter did not have anything in his pockets worth worrying very much about, since his wallet was in Sam's cabin, and he was not particularly concerned about his watch. But he was worried about the liaison ring. If the chance ever came for him to free himself and the kids, it would do them little good unless he could call Sam to his side.

The thin, wiry man removed Carpenter's change purse and knife from his pockets and confiscated his watch, but he either failed to notice the liaison ring or wrote it off as a cheap piece of jewelry not worth taking. Nor did he appear to notice the hearrings in Carpenter's ears. But maybe the kidnappers simply did not care whether he understood what they were saying or not.

After the thin, wiry man secured his hands behind him with a length of white rope provided by the woman, Floyd yanked Carpenter to his feet and shoved him in the direction of the ginkgoes. Deidre and Skip were shoved in the same direction, although their hands had not been tied, and the kidnappers fell in behind the three prisoners.

"I guess," Carpenter said to Skip, who was walking beside him, "that I didn't do you kids much good."

"That's not true, Mr. Carpenter. You did everything you could for us."

"What's the name of the one who searched me?"

"Fred. The tall one's named Floyd—he's the leader. The woman's name is Kate. The fourth one must be in the city. His name is Hugh. He's the worst one."

"How can he be worse than these three?"

"I don't know how, but he is."

"Don't talk!" Kate screamed.

Kate, Floyd, Fred, Hugh. They *sounded* like American names, just as Deidre and Skip did. But Carpenter knew they were not. And he knew something else.

The kidnappers were not mere kidnappers. They were terrorists.

Some distance beyond the frieze of ginkgoes a vehicle was parked on the plain. It made Carpenter think of the Lunar Rover Scott and Irwin had taken to the moon with them and left there, although it was much larger and was of alien design and had pontoons as well as wheels. There were a pair of propellors in the rear that could be lowered for water travel. What it added up to was an amphibious dune buggy.

Skip was hustled into the backseat, and Floyd and Fred seated themselves on either side of him. Kate prodded Deidre and Carpenter into the front seat with her rifle. She then got behind the wheel, attached her rifle to a carrier on the vehicle's side, and started the buggy. She shot the buggy forward, made a violent left turn, and began following Sam's trail, which cut through the plain cover like a secondary road.

The sun was edging above the horizon, and the heat and humidity of a typical Cretaceous day were beginning to set in. But the air was unbelievably fresh, and while the freshness wiped away neither the heat nor the humidity, it made both bearable. By this time Carpenter had figured out how the kidnappers had found the campsite. Sam's illusion field did not function in infrared light, and they must have glided their pteranodons along the line of cliffs employing infrared searchbeams. It had not taken a great deal of brains to figure that the cliffs would be where Carpenter and the kids would head for, but it had taken a few to figure that the triceratank might have an illusion field. Clearly he was not dealing with dimwits.

Kate's right cheek was toward him and he could see it clearly beyond Deidre's buttercup-color hair. He studied the scar. It ran diagonally down from her cheekbone to the edge of her mouth, lending her lips a grotesque upward slant. It must have been made by a knife. Floyd's? Fred's? Hugh's? Whoever its author may have been, she wore the scar proudly. Probably it was her way of telling her civilization to go to hell. A manifestation of her hatred of all things humane. She did not really need it, Carpenter thought. Her eyes bore hatred enough.

Since she did not know Sam was going to come to a halt after five miles, she drove furiously, believing she had to overtake him. The dune buggy lurched this way and that over the uneven ground. Apparently its engine was electric, for it made but little noise. For the most part Sam's trail followed a straight line, but now and then it curved around stands of trees. The dune buggy would never be able to catch up to the reptivehicle if it maintained its present velocity, but it had not been programmed to. Suddenly Kate shouted, "There it is!" and Carpenter saw that Sam, his five miles behind him, had come to a halt in the middle of large expanse of open ground.

Kate barreled the buggy in the reptivehicle's direction. In the backseat Floyd and Fred got their rifles ready. "Maybe it's broke down," Fred said. "Or maybe whoever's driving it's lying in wait for us."

Floyd said, "Slow her down, Kate."

Kate reduced the buggy's speed to a crawl.

About half a mile beyond where Sam was standing was a large herd of ceratopsians. Carpenter regarded it thoughtfully. Although his hands were tied behind him, his fingers were free, and he could easily touch the liaison ring with his thumb. His original intention had been to send Sam off on another five-mile charge, but the presence of the herd proffered a better course of action.

He leaned slightly forward in the seat. His left arm was still numb from the blow it had received from Floyd's rifle, and the numbness had spread down to his fingers. But he did not need his left hand, since his ace card was in his right. He turned the ring gently with his right thumb in search of a circular nodule. When he felt it, he applied pressure.

Sam began "trotting" toward his "brethren."

"Speed her up, Kate!" Floyd shouted. "It's getting away!"

Kate gunned the buggy. Sam continued to "trot." He would keep on "trotting" as long as Carpenter held the nodule in activating position.

The best the buggy could do was match the reptivehicle's speed. In the backseat Floyd leveled his rifle. The left front wheel of the buggy sank into a hole and the beam the rifle emitted stabbed into the sky.

Sam was quite close to the herd now. Its members showed no interest in his approach. All of them were of the genus *Triceratops elatus*, which at this stage of the Cretaceous had superseded previous genera. Would they accept Sam? Carpenter wondered.

They paid no more attention to the buggy than they did to the reptivehicle. Floyd tried another shot. The laserlike beam stabbed a distant tree. "Catch up to him, Kate! Catch up to him!"

"I can't!"

Sam entered the herd.

Its members went on grazing. They were eating shrubs. Carpenter could smell them now. It was a pungent smell. Surely the fact that Sam smelled differently would brand him as an alien. But they went right on grazing. Maybe their combined smell was so intense they could not smell anything else.

He eased up on the nodule, slowing Sam to a "walk." He was unable to see the triceratank now. All he could see were ceratopsians, ceratopsians, ceratopsians. Beside him, Deidre giggled. She had spotted the ring and guessed its true nature.

"Which one is he!" Floyd shouted. "Which one is he!"

Sam had vanished in the crowd.

The dune buggy was now dangerously close to the outskirts of the herd. A big bull turned toward it. The bull was even bigger than Sam. It pawed the ground. Fred aimed his rifle at it but failed to get the shot off because the buggy hit a bump so hard he almost went flying. "Let's get out of here, Kate!"

The big bull pawed the ground again, then charged. Kate made a wild turn on two wheels and headed in the opposite direction. In the backseat Fred and Floyd started shooting at the charging bull, but their beams went wild. The buggy hit another bump, and this time it almost turned over, but Kate did not slow its speed till Floyd shouted, "He's stopped, Kate—slow down!"

Carpenter removed his thumb from the nodule and leaned back in the seat as far as his bound wrists would permit. The terrorists were not going to find Sam today. They would not be able to find him tomorrow either, unless the herd moved, and since they believed Carpenter's "buddy" was behind the wheel they would assume that by then the reptivehicle would be long gone. So the chances were that instead of looking for it, they would try to find out from Carpenter where his "buddy" had taken it.

But this was not a problem he needed to face right away, although he might have to face it soon, for Kate was now heading in an easterly direction. The terrorists were taking their captives to the city.

The cross-country trip to Rimmon was more like a hunting expedition than a trip. The two terrorists in the backseat shot at every animal they saw, and Kate stopped the buggy every now and then so she could shoot too. None of them was a good shot, but the law of averages was on their side. They killed three ornithomimes, two anatosaurs, and five good-sized lizards. When, as the buggy skirted a big pond, they saw a huge alamosaur, they riddled it with their beams till it sank half into the water, a prodigious pile of bleeding flesh. When they came upon a herd of troödons they really had fun. Kate stopped the buggy, and all three blazed away. The creatures were small, ostrichlike, and had knobs of bone on the tops of their heads. The terrorists dropped six before the rest of the herd had sense enough to flee. Floyd and Fred jumped out of the buggy and threw one of the carcasses on the hood. Troödon soup tonight. Later on Kate, after driving the buggy across a shallow creek, killed a dromaeosaur. Dromaeosaurs had huge eyes and relatively large brains, and were referred to as emu reptiles by twentieth-century paleontologists because of the creatures' resemblance to the ostrichlike emu. Kate burned this one's head off.

Deidre looked sick. Carpenter felt sick himself. Clouds of
flying insects began buzzing about the carcass on the hood,
making it even more difficult for Kate to tell where she was
going. She did not seem to mind. At last the city came into
view, the tops of its buildings showing beyond an extensive
stand of cycads. The buildings were chalk white in the late-
morning sunlight, and many of them appeared to be pyramidal.
After the buggy wound its way through the stand of cycads,
Carpenter saw that the city was surrounded by a wall. It was
chalk white, like the buildings.

Far to his left he discerned a huge building built of white
blocks. Adjoining it were several large, horizontal kilns, and
near the kilns stood a big crane. Shrubs grew right up to the
building's sides and surrounded the crane. Neither building nor
crane had been used for a long time. The building had clearly
been a cement factory.

Rimmon had been built of concrete.

But it was a type of concrete such as Carpenter had never
seen before. He studied the wall as the buggy moved in closer.
It had a gloss that suggested polished stone. Then he saw that
in many places the concrete was beginning to crumble.

Skip had said the city had been built almost fifty years ago.
Despite the damp climate, the concrete should have held up
well in that length of time. The fact that it had not indicated
that the builders had had a greater eye for beauty than for
durability.

In a thousand years the concrete would be dust, and the
steel ribs and beams and pillars would rust away to nothing in
the sun and the rain.

Magnolias, like ornamental shrubbery, bloomed along the
wall. Kate paralleled it for a short distance to a big portcullislike
gate. Fred got out, reached through the grille, and struggled
with a horizontal steel bar that locked the gate in place. When
at length it yielded and slid into a socket in the wall, he pushed
the gate open. He closed it after Kate drove through, pulled
the bar back in place, and climbed back into the buggy.

The wall proved to be at least twenty feet thick. It brought
to Carpenter's mind the wall that once had surrounded ancient
Babylon. This wall would not be much more durable.

The buggy was now inside the city. The pyramidal buildings

Carpenter had seen from a distance were the dominant structures, but they had three sides instead of four. The buildings that were not pyramidal were square, but they achieved a pyramidal effect by means of narrow terraces on each of their successive floors. The windows in the tetrahedral structures were triangular, those in the square structures, square. Not only was Martian architecture monotonous, it was simplistic. Each window was bisected by a narrow vertical bar, or strip, but no glass was in evidence. The square structures ranged from five to eight stories in height. Since the windows in the tetrahedral structures were not positioned in straight lines, it was impossible to tell how many stories were involved, but the buildings were considerably taller than the square ones.

Three-sided pyramids . . . Were they tied in with the gigantic ones *Mariner 9* would photograph on Mars millions of years in the future? Carpenter found it hard to believe. The three-sided pyramids of Elysium surely could not have been built this long ago.

Kate was driving down a wide avenue. Now she turned into a side street. Carpenter wished he were driving Sam. He wished this for quite a number of reasons, but at the moment he wished it primarily because of the holographs Sam's holo cameras could take. A documentary of a Martian city in the Upper Cretaceous. It would make NAPS' eyes pop. But naturally NAPS wouldn't believe it was a Martian city. The paleontologists would fish around for another more down-to-Earth answer, and if they could not find one they would make one up.

The street along which the buggy was moving was paved with a coarser form of concrete than that used in the buildings and the wall. It was cracked in many places. Kate made another turn. Carpenter tried to commit the route to memory. He hoped Deidre and Skip were trying too. He had a hunch they would fare much better than he.

Kate drove deeper and deeper into the city. Cycads grew in small plots of ground along the streets and avenues. Occasionally Carpenter glimpsed sections of the wall beyond vistas of buildings and realized that the city was not truly a city, that at most it could have harbored no more than ten thousand people—not even that many if some of the buildings, as they more or less had to have been, were warehouses, business places, and the like. But "city" stuck in his mind. It would be unromantic, he thought, to call such an exotic place a mere village.

When, some distance up the street along which Kate was driving, he saw a pedestrian, he thought for a moment that all the colonists had not left after all. Then he realized that the pedestrian must be the fourth terrorist. Out, perhaps, for a morning walk. When the man saw the approaching buggy, he waited for it, then, after tossing aside a flagon he was carrying, jumped onto the running board. He was built like a sumo wrestler and had neither hair nor beard. His coveralls were like those of the other terrorists, but much dirtier. He had eyes like little blue agates and his lips were thick and rubbery. He reeked of alcohol.

He leaned across Carpenter and smiled at Deidre. "So they brought my pretty back!" he said in a strikingly high voice.

Deidre leaned as far away from him as she could. There was outraged pride in her eyes—and terror. Carpenter bent forward, shoving the terrorist away. The terrorist smiled at him. Warmly. "And look who else they brought!"

"His buddy got away with the tank," Fred said. "We're going to have fun getting him to tell where he took it."

"He ain't no Greater Martian. He ain't any kind of Martian at all."

"We don't know what he is yet, Hugh," Kate said, "but we're going to find out."

Hugh patted Carpenter's cheek. "I can't wait."

The terrorists' safe house was one of the square, terraced buildings. When Kate stopped before it, Carpenter noted that it was five stories high. It had a doorway large enough for her to back the dune buggy inside. Floyd poked Carpenter's back with his rifle. "Out." Kate went round and opened the door. When the buggy was empty, Fred closed the building's door. Despite its alien design, it was much like a twentieth-century overhead garage door.

The ground floor consisted of a single large room. A helical stairway rose from its center. Miscellaneous objects were scattered everywhere, a clear indication the terrorists had thoroughly canvassed the city. Near the door was a long wooden bench which was loaded with tools the colonists had probably been in too much of a hurry to take with them. There were bales of wire, coils of rope, heaps of clothing, a conglomeration of alien equipment; dishes, pots, pans. Standing against the farther wall was what looked like a kitchen stove. Next to it was a cupboard, and not far from the cupboard was an inbuilt sink overflowing with dirty dishes. In front of the cupboard was a six-legged wooden table with four oddly shaped chairs around it. Not far from it a section of the floor had been cleared to make room for four filthy oblong pads. The blankets tangled on top of them indicated they were beds.

There were windows in only two of the walls, and the light coming through them provided the room's only illumination. The sun was directly overhead by this time, and the light barely reached the limestone wall on Carpenter's left, so he did not at first notice the mural. When he finally did, he stared at it. He saw fields and hills, rich green, and a deep-blue sky. He saw blue rivers that managed somehow to look like canals. He saw a little village in a green valley, and its buildings were like the buildings of Rimmon. And beyond the village he saw the gigantic three-sided pyramids and the immense four-sided rectangular pyramid *Mariner 9* would photograph in the far, far future. And he knew he was seeing part of the eastern section of the Elysium quadrangle, not as *Mariner 9* would see it, but as it was now, when Mars knew life.

Kate's rifle dug into his back. "Upstairs!"

He looked at the kids. They were looking at him. Desperation had darkened the blueness of their eyes. "Hey, you guys— I'll get you out of this somehow."

"Shut up and move!" Kate screamed. He picked his way through the terrorists' plunder to the stairway. He wanted to turn and tear Kate's rifle from her grasp, but he knew he would be dead before the turn was half completed. He gave the kids a final glance over his shoulder. It was meant to reassure them but he knew it was tinged with the same desperation that resided in their eyes. Then he preceded the woman up the stairs.

Chapter 5

CARPENTER CLIMBED FOUR flights of stairs, the muzzle of Kate's rifle nudging his back every step he took. The stairway was concrete. It had a fine, smooth finish, but it was beginning to show signs of wear. The layout of the building suggested that it had once functioned as a hotel. The entire ground floor could have comprised the lobby. The stairwell was octagonal and surrounded on each of the successive floors by an octagonal balcony which in each instance, judging from the number of doors, gave access to eight rooms. Only the doors were painted—a pale, lifeless blue. The bare concrete of the walls, floors, and ceilings lent the impression of polished stone. Unfortunately, the "polished stone" had cracked in many places and had flaked away in others.

But for all Carpenter knew, all of the square buildings in the city might be laid out in the same way as this one, and instead of once functioning as a hotel, the safe house might have been a typical apartment house.

The thought of all the structural steel that must have been transported from Mars to Earth during the building of the city awed him. Well over 74,000,000 years before the Russians launched *Sputnik* a race twentieth-century Earth people had never seriously imagined transported the steel skeleton of an entire city millions of miles through space to the Age of Reptiles!

Well, no, not the skeleton of a city, but the skeleton of a citylike village. But it was still a marvelous accomplishment. And consider the stupendous number of other items that also had been transported. And all the people.

But they had defeated the transportation problem in one respect: They had made their cement on Earth, using limestone from the cliffs, probably, and Earth clay and shale. And Earth ingredients too must have constituted at least part of the magical mixture that had given their concrete the aspect of polished stone.

On the fifth floor Kate opened the door to one of the rooms. The door's paint had flaked away in many places, and Carpenter saw that the door was made of steel. If all the doors in the city were also steel . . . He was awed again. But his awe was tempered by the remembrance of the desperation in Deidre's and Skip's eyes.

Greater Mars, for all its logistical greatness, was not going to free the two kids from the terrorists. The task lay on his doorstep alone.

Kate shoved him into the room beyond the doorway. Floyd had followed them upstairs, and he covered Carpenter with his rifle after Kate set hers aside. She ordered Carpenter to lie down and then proceeded to bind his ankles with a length of plastic rope she had brought with her. It was a long length of rope, and she wound it halfway up to his knees before tying it. He hoped she would not inspect the sloppy job Fred had done in securing his wrists. She did not, and after giving him a parting kick in the ribs, departed with Floyd, closing the door behind her. He had not noticed a lock on the door, or a knob either, but he heard a cold, uncompromising *click*.

The room had one window. The sun had passed meridian

by this time, and a small parallelogram of light lay on the concrete floor. There was nothing in the room except dust. Its walls and ceiling laughed at him. They had been painted pale green years ago, but much of the paint had peeled away.

He was lying on his back in the middle of the floor. By repeatedly doubling and straightening his legs he propelled himself to the outer wall and hunched himself into a sitting position near the window. The numbness had left his left arm, and he began working his wrists back and forth. Fred had left considerable play. If there were Boy Scouts in Greater Mars, he had never been one.

While trying to free his hands, Carpenter studied the rope Kate had used to bind his legs. He estimated its diameter to be about half an inch. He had a hunch it was unbreakable, or nearly so. This pleased him. So did the amount of rope she had used. He had a half-formed plan.

He could smell the rich green smell of the plain and occasionally he heard the faraway screams and grunts and screeches of theropods and sauropods and ornithopods. He also heard a distant murmur, and he was sure it was the sound of the sea— the inland sea that stretched upward in a long arm across much of western North America. The sea the colonists had feared to fish in. Their reluctance to cast off in fishing boats was certainly understandable. They would have had to cope with long-necked elasmosaurs, short-necked pliosaurs, lizardlike tylosaurs and gigantic mosasaurs. This was unfortunate, for there were plenty of fish to be had. At this stage of the Cretaceous, teleosts abounded.

The parallelogram of sunlight gradually elongated as it inched across the floor. Carpenter's wrists were beginning to hurt. The rope seemed to have no resilience. He had had nothing to drink since the cocoa he had drunk that morning, and his mouth and throat were dry. As the day dragged on, they became parched. It was hot in the room, and even the little effort he needed to expend to move his wrists back and forth caused sweat to break out on his forehead. The sweat kept running down into his eyes, irritating them. He kept his mind on Deidre and Skip. He did not believe that the terrorists would harm them. He would not let himself believe that they would. Their eagerness to get the kids back proved they still needed their voices for more radio messages to Greater Mars. No, so long as they needed the kids' voices, they would not harm them. But how about afterward?

A quantity of desperation invested itself in his efforts to free his hands. His wrists were raw by this time, but he no longer felt the pain. He kept trying to reassure himself. Deidre was only a child; so was Skip. Surely even terrorists would draw the line at killing mere children. Evidently they had not yet physically harmed them—Skip would have said so if they had. But maybe they just had not gotten around to it. Maybe the intention was there. He remembered the blow Kate had aimed at Deidre. He shuddered. Then he remembered the way Hugh had looked at her. He shuddered again. If the Ku had seeded Mars, why had they not culled their seeds? That way there would be no Floyd and Fred and Kate and Hugh. He began to hate the Ku although he doubted their reality. The rope around his wrists had loosened a little more, but he could not even begin to pull his hands free. The parallelogram of light had reached the farther wall and was edging up it. He listened for sounds from within the building but heard none. What could the terrorists be doing? Had they gone to their spaceship? Skip had said it was about a mile south of the city. Perhaps they had gone to it and taken the kids with them and were radioing Greater Mars. If this were so, and they were forcing Deidre and Skip to speak to their parents, they might not have any use for the kids afterward, and—

Carpenter focused his attention on his wrists and shut all other thoughts from his mind. It would do neither him nor the kids any good if he went crazy worrying about them. The parallelogram of light was now touching the ceiling and was beginning to shrink. He tried again to pull his hands free. In vain. His mouth and throat had turned into blotting paper. He resumed working his wrists back and forth. At length he saw that the parallelogram of light had disappeared. Grayness now filled the room.

Back and forth, back and forth, back and forth. The grayness gave way to darkness. He continued to try to free his hands. They were chafed to the point where they had begun to bleed. Suddenly he heard footsteps on the balcony and stopped moving his wrists. A crack of yellow light had appeared beneath the door. There was a click, and the door opened, and a figure carrying a small lantern stepped into the room. It was Kate.

She closed the door behind her and set the lantern on the floor. It was unlike any lantern Carpenter had ever seen. The source of its light made him think of a large yellow egg. The "egg" rested on a nest of multicolored wires to which the ends of a delicate metal handle were attached. It filled the room with warm, mellow light. Kate sat down on the other side of the lantern, doubled her legs, and crossed her feet. She withdrew a pair of hearrings from a breast pocket and attached them to her ears. "Where're you and your buddy from?"

"Earth-future," Carpenter said.

She blinked. Then: "Well, we know you're not a Martian and we know that this planet has no human life. The seven other planets of the solar system are dead, which means that if you and your buddy are from another world it must be part of another star system, and that would mean you, your buddy, and the grotesque tank traveled light-years to get here in a spaceship you've hidden somewhere. That's pretty hard to believe. Martian scientists say that time travel is possible, so maybe you *are* from the future."

"How do you know I'm not a Martian?" Carpenter asked.

"We just know, is all. How far from the future are you from?"

"Farther than you'd believe."

"What're you doing here?"

"Holographing this phase of the past."

"Where did your buddy go?"

"You saw yourself where he went. He joined the ceratopsians."

"You must have a base somewhere. That's where he went, isn't it?"

"When I heard you outside on the balcony," Carpenter said, "I was sure you were bringing me something to eat."

"Maybe you've got more than one buddy. If you have, we want to know where all of them are. And we want your tank."

"Even a crust of bread would have helped," Carpenter said. "A sip of wine would have been welcome too."

Kate leaned forward slightly. The mellow light from the lantern had softened the line of her scar but it had turned her brown eyes to pale orange. "We want your tank, and we will get it."

"I'll trade it to you for the kids."

"Why are you interested in the kids?"

"Because they're kids and they're helpless. What're you going to make the Greater Mars Kingdom do to get them back?"

"They'll never get them back no matter what they do."

"The boy is about nine, the girl about eleven. The only crime they're guilty of is having been born rich. If it's necessary for you to punish the Greater Mars Establishment because of some wrong you think it's done you or because you just plain hate it, then punish it. But when you're done, give the two kids back."

Kate grinned, and the grin extended upward through the scar to her cheekbone. "You're part of the Establishment, aren't you? The one in the age you come from."

"No. It's unaware of me. I hate it as much as you hate yours. But I can't destroy it any more than you can destroy yours, and I wouldn't even if I could, because another, possibly a worse one, would take its place."

"It wouldn't be a worse one if it were properly engineered."

"People who destroy Establishments aren't qualified to engineer anything. And all they ever really want is the power they pretend to hate."

"It's fools like you," Kate said, "who make Establishments possible."

"I should think," Carpenter said, changing the subject, "that if you really want my—our—tank, you could have found it with your flyabouts by this time."

"If we tried to, your buddy would only jump it back in time the way you or he did yesterday."

Again Carpenter realized he was not dealing with dimwits. Not only had the terrorists guessed where he and the kids had been hiding, they had also figured out how he had eluded them. "Well, anyway," he said, "I know now why you so readily believed I'm from the future—and why you want the repti-vehicle."

Kate stood up. "We don't really care where you're from." She picked up the lantern. "You got a little breathing time this afternoon because we had to prepare our next message to the

Kingdom. Tonight you'll get a little more because we want
you to think about what's going to happen if you don't tell us
what we want to know. I'll be back early in the morning. If
by then you don't tell us where your buddy took the tank, I'll
burn the little girl's eyes out."

The room became tomb dark after she closed the door and
clicked the lock into place. Part of the darkness came from
Carpenter's horrified reaction to her threat and the sick certainty
she would carry it out. This part remained after his retinas
adjusted to the ordinary part and enabled him to see the room
dimly in the starlight coming through the window.

He returned furiously to work on his wrist bonds, trying to
pull one hand free and then the other. Both hands were bleeding
now. He had no sensation of the passage of time and was
startled when moonlight joined the starlight in the room. Since
the window faced west, the moon must have passed the meridian.

The blood finally helped him to free his hands. It was like
oil. When his right hand slipped free, he held it before his eyes
and stared at it as though he had never seen it before. Then he
held up his left hand. It was as blood-smeared and as strange
as his right.

He untied the knots Fred had made in the wrist rope. They
were housewife knots; he wondered how they had ever held.
Next he untied the knots Kate had made in the rope binding
his legs. They were housewife knots too. After unwinding the
rope, he stood up and walked around the room till the tingling
in his legs and feet went away. Then he stretched out the two
lengths of rope on the floor. They seemed to be the same kind,
and his fingers told him they had the same diameter. The shorter
length was about two and a half feet long, the longer one, about
eleven. He went over to the window and looked down. There
were cycads growing near the building in what had probably
been a small park. They were not quite as high as the window.
The narrow terraces on each floor made each successive story
slightly smaller than the one below. The highest terrace ran a
few feet beneath the window ledge. The next one down was
about twelve feet below the ledge. He had more than enough
rope.

He realized that he was trembling. He had been terrified that there might not be enough. When his hands steadied he felt the vertical strip that bisected the window, since the star- and the moonlight were not bright enough for him to see it clearly. His fingers encountered small nodules. The strips that comprised the rest of the window frame were flush with the square aperture, and his fingers found small nodules protruding from them too. He had a hunch that the frame was a projector for a force field, but his concern was with the sturdiness of the strip, not with the frame's function. The strip was about an inch square. He gripped it with both hands and pulled on it. It did not give. He pulled harder. It remained firmly fixed in place.

He hoped the strips in the other windows were equally solid.

He tied the ropes together, employing a tight square knot, obtaining a single length of about thirteen feet. Then he coiled the rope and slung the coil around his left shoulder. During his descent he would have to look into every room in case Deidre and Skip might be imprisoned in one of them, and before he even began the descent he would have to look into the other rooms on the fifth floor. It was possible the kids were still in the ground-floor room, but he had no way of knowing this, so the only sensible course of action would be to check the upper stories on his way down.

He was reasonably sure each room had a window. His mental picture of the building's facade showed three windows on each floor, except the first. So the chances were that there were three windows to a floor on each of the other sides. This meant that the corner rooms had two windows apiece, and the rooms in between, such as the room he was in now, one.

Leaning through the window, he looked down. The pinnate leaves of the cycads had been tinted argent by the moon. He raised his eyes. The windows of the next building stared back at him. To his right he could see the street that the safe house faced on. It was tinted argent too. He looked at the moon. It made him think of the campfire and the kids.

The odds had it that the terrorists were still inside the safe house. Slipping through the window, he lowered his feet to the terrace below its ledge. It was about eighteen inches wide, a perfect pathway for a former mountaineer such as himself.

He began moving sideways along it in a clockwise direction, facing the wall. Before each sideways step he explored the terrace with his left foot in case the concrete had crumbled. When he came to the window of the corner room he peered inside. It was deserted.

He rounded the corner of the building. He was cut off from the moonlight now, and all he had to see by was the light of the stars. It was a benign, soft light. He saw that there were three windows and was certain now that all the sides of the building presented the same face.

He passed the other window of the corner room and peered into the next room. It too was deserted. Continuing his circuit of the building, he found that the entire fifth floor was vacant.

It was time to begin the descent.

He was now at the window of the corner room south of the room in which he had been imprisoned. He pulled hard on the bisecting strip. It did not budge. After uncoiling the rope, he tied one end of it to the strip, employing a mountaineer's knot like a timber hitch. It would not give while there was a strain on the rope but could be worked free from below when the rope was slack. He began lowering himself hand over hand to the next terrace. Above him, despite the brightness of the moon, he could see the stars. The Cretaceous stars. He made out the orange pinprick of Mars. He found it strange to see the planet way up there in the sky. Since entering the Martian city he had half believed he was on Mars. Ancient Mars of the rich green hills and valleys, of the rivers that looked like canals. Of the tetrahedral pyramids that would endure for over 74,000,000 years, and perhaps forever.

The windows of the building, despite the slight shrinkage of each successive floor, were positioned one above the other, and to reach the next terrace down he had to lower himself past the window just above it. It was a calculated risk. The absence of any light emanating from the aperture reassured him, but he did not relax till he came opposite the window and saw that there was no one in the room beyond.

Reaching the terrace, he let the rope grow slack, then worked the knot free. After recoiling and reshouldering the rope, he started moving clockwise around the building again. He found more deserted rooms on the west and north sides. Then, rounding the corner to the east side, he saw light coming from the far corner window—light that he had failed to notice from above because he had been facing the wall.

He slowed his pace, careful not to make a sound. He looked into the intermediate room, found it deserted. When he had almost reached the lighted window, he stopped and peered past its edge into the room beyond. Kate and Floyd and Fred were sitting around a six-legged table upon which stood Kate's lantern, or one exactly like it, a flagon, and four cups. Hugh was standing near the doorway, holding another lantern. Apparently he was about to leave. There was no sign of Deidre and Skip. The open doors of a floor-to-ceiling cupboard revealed shelves lined with flagons similar to the one standing on the table.

The terrorists' private bar?

Carpenter pulled his head back out of sight. The terrorists were arguing. He found he could distinguish the four voices from one another. Floyd's was coarse and grating, Fred's slightly hoarse, Hugh's like an Irish tenor's. Kate's, of course, stood out all by itself.

Hugh said, "I don't see what the hurry is. Kirk won't call till the middle of the night."

"You just get out there anyway in case he calls sooner!" Floyd said.

"He won't," Hugh said.

"You get out there anyway!" Floyd said.

The door slammed.

"You shouldn't have sent him," Kate said. "He's drunk. He's been drinking all day. He's liable to drive the buggy into a bog."

"You don't like the idea of him going, go yourself!" Floyd said.

"You've no right to expect a woman to drive out to that ship in the dark!"

"Then shut up, Kate!"

"With a million starz on the line, Floyd, you send a drunk to man the radio!" Kate said.

"Cool it, you two. Hugh'll get Kirk's message all right," Fred said.

"Why can't he radio us in the daytime? What difference

does it make to him on Mars whether it's night or not on Earth?"
Kate asked.

"Kirk's funny," Fred said.

"Do you think they paid off?" Kate asked.

"They'd better have!" Floyd said.

"If they did," Fred said, "maybe we should just settle for
the starz and forget about telling them to hand out more goodies
to the poor and to disband the Intelligence Agency and to double
welfare payments and all that other stuff we're going to tell
them to do tomorrow."

"You're sick, Fred," Kate said.

"I can maybe see the point in making them disband the
Intelligence Agency. That could do us some good. But what
good is it going to do us to have them shell out more food to
the poor and double welfare? The only thing that's going to
do us any real good is the million starz."

"We can make them pay through the nose, Fred, in all the
ways we want to when we put those brats on the air again
tomorrow, and that's what we're going to do!"

"Maybe they don't want the princess and the prince back
as bad as the two of you think they do, Floyd. The king's got
plenty of nieces and nephews who can succeed him."

"You don't know anything, Fred," Kate said. "Tradition
says the oldest child, regardless of sex, is next in line for the
throne. That's what rules Greater Mars—tradition. Not the
king, not the Parliament, not the First Speaker. Tradition. There's
never been a time in the history of the Kingdom when a son
or a daughter wasn't available. The lack of one would bring
the whole country to its knees. So the Parliament and the First
Speaker will do anything to get the prince and princess back.
Anything!"

Floyd laughed. "Only to not get them back anyway!"

"I want to take care of the princess myself," Kate said. "The
dirty little aristocrat!"

Carpenter shuddered.

The conversation shifted from the kids to him. Kate had
already informed Floyd and Fred that Carpenter claimed to be
from the future, and apparently they had believed it as readily
as Kate had. No doubt for the same reason—Sam's jumpback
in time. But none of them thought he was from the far future.

They talked in terms of a thousand to two thousand years. This led them to conclude that the Ku were going to seed Earth with human beings very soon, despite its geological instability.

They went on to speculate on where his buddy might have taken the tank. Fred said probably into the highlands. Kate suggested that maybe he had taken it into the future. Floyd said he did not think so. Kate then said they would find out tomorrow morning, because Carpenter—they referred to him as "the Man from the Future"—would tell them rather than let her burn the princess's eyes out. She went on to wonder why his buddy hadn't time-jumped the tank when they were chasing it and concluded he had been unaware they had guessed its ability and had not wanted to let them see it disappear. She and Floyd and Fred then started talking about how they were going to spend the ransom money. It appeared that each of them was going to buy a host of expensive items—the same sort of items, Carpenter suspected, that the members of the Establishment, whom they despised, set so much store by.

He had heard all he wanted to hear. Rather than risk being spotted passing the window, he circled the building counterclockwise to the south side and looked into the final fourth-floor room—the intermediate one on the other side of the terrorists' meeting place. Finding it deserted, he descended to the third-floor terrace.

He began circling the building clockwise again, listening for the sound of the dune buggy. By now Hugh should have driven it out into the street. Evidently he had not, which meant he was still in the safe house. Reaching the north side, which faced the street, Carpenter looked down, expecting momentarily to see the buggy emerge from the doorway. It did not. An icy tremor ran the gamut of his backbone. At this point he noticed that there was light coming from the middle window.

He had a bad habit of thinking the worst, and he did so now, this time with justification, for as he neared the window he heard an Irish tenor voice say, "You can't get away, my pretty." Looking through the window, he saw Hugh standing in the middle of the room. He had hung his egg lantern on a wall peg, and it filled the room with mellow light. The room was slightly smaller than the one Carpenter had been imprisoned in, but despite the mellowness of the light, no less ugly.

Skip was tucked away in a corner, tightly bound. Deidre's
bonds lay at her feet. They had been cut, but Carpenter saw
no sign of a knife. She had backed against the right-hand wall.
Her blouse had been torn away and her chemise had been ripped
down the middle. Her face was as white as it had been when
Carpenter had first seen her in the ginkgo tree, and her autumn-
aster eyes were filled with horror. Hugh took a step toward
her. Another. Saliva oozed from the corner of his rubbery
mouth. She tried to back farther away but could not. The walls
of the room were painted blue. In Carpenter's gaze the blueness
turned to red. He removed the coil of rope from his shoulder.
He did not even notice when it slipped from his fingers and
fell down the building's side to the street. He had eyes only
for the room.

    For Hugh.

Chapter 6

Hugh did not see Carpenter slip through the window. His eyes were focused on Deidre.

He did not see him till Carpenter stepped between him and Deidre. Deidre did not see him till then either. She gave a small, soft cry.

"He has a knife, Mr. Carpenter!" Skip shouted.

If Hugh did, it was hidden from sight. Carpenter was not worried in any case. It was unlikely Hugh would bother with a knife this early in the proceedings when confronted with so relatively puny an opponent.

The lust in his agate eyes had transmuted to rage. But the rage was as skimmed milk compared to Carpenter's. Carpenter's rage was cold and calculating. He knew he had to let Hugh make the first move. He might have Martian muscles, but he was half again Carpenter's size.

You always had to let the bigger man attack so you could use his weight against him.

Hugh began mouthing words Carpenter's hearrings could not cope with. Curse words, probably, that had no Anglo-American equivalent.

They must be violent curse words indeed.

Abruptly Hugh lunged across the several feet that separated him from Carpenter. Carpenter waited till all of the big man's weight was on his right leg, then kicked his right knee. Hugh gave an agonized grunt and fell like a mountain. Carpenter then aimed a kick for his throat. Hugh seized his foot, twisted it and brought him to the floor, and then the man-mountain was on top of him.

Carpenter squirmed beneath the crushing weight. Thick fingers found his throat. Their strength appalled him. Much had been affirmed about the lighter gravity of Mars-future, but Hugh was from Mars-present. Skip's argument that there was more gravity on Mars-future than Earthmen thought would not hold up, but his speculation that Mars' gravity at this point in time was stronger than it would be had been authenticated. Though Carpenter had only come up against the strength of Hugh's hands, it had given him an inkling of how strong the man really was, and he simply could not be that strong unless his weight on Mars equalled his weight on Earth.

This was a scientific impossibility. It was also an ineluctable fact.

Carpenter could not break Hugh's grip, so in desperation he brought his knee up into the man's groin. Hugh grunted, and his fingers relaxed. Carpenter twisted free and squirmed from beneath the man-mountain. He staggered to his feet. Hugh lumbered to his. His jaw was wide open, and Carpenter did what he should have done in the first place: He threw a right cross. But he was off balance and the blow was weak and landed on Hugh's temple. Nevertheless Hugh felt it. Carpenter next threw a left. Hugh blocked it with his right forearm, but his left arm was still hanging at his side and he was wide open for another right. "The knife! The knife!" Skip shouted. "It's in his sleeve!" But Carpenter had already thrown the right. The knife appeared as if by magic in Hugh's right hand. It descended toward Carpenter's right arm as Carpenter's right fist arrowed toward Hugh's jaw. The fist won the race, but a split second later the blade sank into Carpenter's flesh just above his forearm, severing the brachial artery. Instantly blood began spurting from the wound.

Carpenter knew he had little time left. His right arm was now useless, but Hugh had been badly stunned by the blow. Although he was still standing, his eyes were glazed. Carpenter connected with a left. Right on the button. But his strength was draining from him, and the blow lacked authority. He threw another left. Hugh swayed. Carpenter was now standing in his own blood. Another left. Hugh continued to sway. "For God's sake—fall!" Carpenter whispered, and swung again. At last the man-mountain crumpled to the floor, the knife still gripped in his hand.

Carpenter knew he had to stop the bleeding fast. He tried to unbuckle his belt, but he had only one hand to work with. Then Deidre was at his side. She unbuckled it for him, pulled it free from his trousers, wound it around his upper right arm, and buckled it into a tight tourniquet. "Quick, Pumpkin," he whispered, "cut Skip loose." But she had already pulled the knife from Hugh's hand and was hurrying toward her brother. She cut his bonds, then dropped the knife and searched for her blouse. She found it and put it on. In an instant she was back at Carpenter's side.

He palpated the liaison ring with his left forefinger. He hoped none of the nodules had been accidentally depressed when he hit Hugh. The home nodule was a tiny hex. Finding it, he pushed it down. He had never thought he would be in such desperate need of Sam.

Skip had now joined his sister. His delicate features were a study in anguish. He looked at the cut on Carpenter's arm. It had stopped bleeding. He looked up into Carpenter's face. "Are you all right, Mr. Carpenter? Are you all right?"

"I'm fine," Carpenter lied. "Let's go, you guys. We've got to make it outside the city. Sam is on the way." The room tipped before his eyes. He willed himself to remain standing. "We've got to hurry. The other three are upstairs and may have heard us. Get the lantern, Skip."

Deidre pushed the door open and they stepped out onto the

balcony. The sound of voices and footsteps came from the floor above. Looking up the stairs, Carpenter saw Kate's face in the lantern light. He heard her sharp-edged voice. "He got away! He's got the kids with him!"

Down the stairs, Skip in the lead, Deidre just behind him, Carpenter bringing up the rear. The sound of furious footsteps from above. The lantern swung wildly in Skip's hand. Had there been rifles in the room where the three terrorists had been twisting the threads of fate over their booze? Carpenter wondered. He had not seen any. They would be useless on the helical stairway in any case.

The second floor. In Carpenter's gaze the stairway twisted more than it should. He forced it to realign itself. The big ground-floor room. "The buggy!" Skip cried. "Let's take their buggy!"

It was parked just within the garage door. Skip set the lantern on the floor and climbed behind the wheel. Carpenter headed for the building's door. He had seen Floyd close it, so he knew it was not automatic. There was a deep groove near its base. Slipping the fingers of his left hand into it, he pulled upward. The door did not budge. Deidre joined him and slipped her fingers into the groove beside his. They lifted together. Either she was stronger than she looked or more of Carpenter's strength remained than he had thought, for the door slid smoothly upward.

By this time Skip had brought the buggy's motor to life. The three terrorists were now pounding down the final flight of stairs, Kate in the lead. They were unarmed. The light of the lantern had illuminated the entire room and Carpenter saw that their rifles were leaning against the kitchen wall.

Deidre was pushing him toward the buggy. "You get in first, Pumpkin," he said. After she climbed into the front seat he picked up the lantern with his left hand and heaved it with what little strength he had left toward the four filthy beds. It struck the floor just before them, exploded, and sent fingers of flames arcing into the tangled blankets. The terrorists came to a startled stop at the foot of the stairs. Kate recovered first. "Floyd! Fred! Close the door so they can't get out! I'll get the guns." She headed for the kitchen, skirting the flames. Floyd and Fred began running toward the door.

Deidre had grabbed Carpenter's arm. She half dragged him
into the front seat beside her. Skip gunned the motor, and
before Floyd and Fred were halfway across the floor, zoomed
the buggy out into the street.

The city. It had an unreal aspect in Carpenter's eyes. The
buildings swayed, the streets wavered, the cycads waved their
pinnate leaves. The sky was also unreal. The stars whirled, the
moon was a dancing mellow disk.

Angrily he brought the buildings and the streets and the
cycads back into proper focus. He cemented the stars in place
and put the moon back on an even keel.

Beside him, Deidre loosened the tourniquet, then tightened
it again. Odd that the Princess of Greater Mars should be
ministering to a mere truck driver. What looked like a tiny star
glistened momentarily on her cheek. If he had not known better
he would have sworn it was a tear.

He tried to remember the route Kate had taken to the safe
house. He could not. The streets and avenues were a labyrinth.
But not to Skip. He rounded corners and zoomed around curves
as though he had been driving in the city all his life. Now that
the safe house was far behind, he had turned on the buggy's
head beams. Presently the gate came into view.

Skip stopped before it and got out. Deidre slid out the
driver's side, and they began trying to shove the big steel bar
with which Fred had struggled back into its socket. By this
time Carpenter was partway out of the buggy. Then he saw he
would not have to get the rest of the way out because the bar
at last had yielded to the kids' efforts. They swung the gate
open. Carpenter slumped back into the seat and Deidre slid in
beside him from the driver's side. Back behind the wheel, Skip
gunned the buggy out of the city.

"Sam," Carpenter said, wondering why his voice sounded
so far away. "He should show up any second."

Skip veered slightly to the left, and they entered the stand
of cycads the buggy had passed through on the way to the city.
He veered more to the left and followed a course parallel to
the city's wall. Carpenter wanted to explain that the reason
Sam would be there any second was that when the home nodule
of the liaison ring was activated, the reptivehicle traveled at

full speed toward the ring's location, but for some reason the words in his mind were unable to cover the distance to his tongue. The explanation would have proved unnecessary in any case, for as the buggy came to the end of the stand and emerged into the star and the moonlight, a familiar shape lumbered into sight.

"Sam!" Skip cried, braking the buggy. "Oh, boy!"

Deidre climbed across Carpenter's lap and helped him get out of the vehicle. The moon was jumping up and down again, and again the stars were whirling. Sam seemed to sway in the moonlight. Why didn't Skip get out of the buggy too? *Skip*, Carpenter tried to shout, *come on*! But the words failed to make it to his tongue.

The boy drove the buggy forward a short distance and peered into the swath cut by the head beams. Then he gunned the motor and the buggy hurtled straight ahead. *Skip!* Carpenter tried to shout, but his lips made no sound. Then the boy jumped out of the driver's seat to the ground, landed on his feet, and did a neat somersault. The buggy continued to hurtle forward. Then it stopped. Abruptly. Carpenter saw that it was mired in the middle of a bog.

Skip came running back. "I remembered that place from when we looked for the spaceship. It's quicksand."

The buggy's pontoons helped a little, but not much. It began to sink. Its head beams winked out. It became knee-high in the moonlight. Suddenly there was a loud *PLOOP*! and it vanished from sight.

Maybe if the NAPS' field workers did some more digging they'd find the petrified chassis of a true foreign import.

Sam had come right up to Carpenter's side like a great big dog eager to be petted. Carpenter pressed the hex, releasing the reptivehicle from remote control. Then he found the built-in handle of the passenger-side door and disengaged the lock. The door swung open. "I'll drive him, Mr. Carpenter," Skip said. "I know how."

Carpenter did not say anything. He sagged against Sam's threads. He felt hands supporting him, but the hands were not strong enough, and he continued to sag. Presently he felt the ground beneath his back. He looked up into the sky. It had become a merry-go-round. The moon had turned into a silvery horse. Round and round it went. He tried to climb on it the way he used to climb on such horses when he was a kid, but it slipped away, and the carrousel spun faster and faster and finally it spun so fast that it arrowed off into the darkness and disappeared.

_____Chapter

_____ 7

CARPENTER WAS LYING in a church, upon a bier. He was certain he had died.

No, not a church. A cathedral.

On either side, white pillars comprised of big square blocks of limestone stacked one upon the other rose up to a lofty vaulted ceiling which also appeared to be limestone and from which light was reflected down into the vast nave below.

He was unable to see the cathedral's walls. Probably because they were too far away.

Yes, he was definitely dead, for there was an angel sitting beside him. She was crying.

She had a bowl on her lap and a spoon in her hand. The bowl contained chicken soup. He could tell by the smell.

His bier had been propped up at one end so that even though he was lying on it he was in a semisitting position. Someone had covered him with blankets.

The spoon in the angel's hand touched his lips and he swallowed its contents. Yes, it was chicken soup. It warmed his throat. He swallowed another spoonful.

Why would an angel be feeding him chicken soup if he was dead?

Everything sort of faded away.

When he opened his eyes again the angel was still there. She was no longer crying, but her eyes were wet. They had the blueness of autumn asters after a September rain.

She still had the bowl of soup on her lap. Or perhaps it was a different bowl. He did not know how long he had been away. Whether it was a different bowl or not, he knew by the smell that it contained chicken soup. A spoon touched his lips and he swallowed a small mouthful. It was good soup. It was the best soup he had ever tasted.

The nave of the cathedral was more distinct now. A considerable distance before him he could see one of its walls. It looked more like a big pile of rocks than a wall. To the left of the rocks was a vine-covered opening. It must be afternoon or morning outside, for the sunlight coming through the interstices of the vines had painted arabesques on the floor.

Such an odd entrance for a cathedral!

The spoon again. He swallowed some more chicken soup. Then a small container of milk, with a straw in it, appeared. He sucked on the straw. The milk must be from Sam's refrigerator, for it was cold.

Sam?

Yes. Sam. His triceratank.

He heard a murmuring sound. It was like the purling of a brook.

He went away again.

When he came back he saw two faces. One was that of the angel, the other of a boy. He recognized the boy. His name was Skip. Then he recognized the angel. She was the Princess of Greater Mars.

Was this her palace?

More chicken soup. Spoonful by spoonful. And more milk. He drank half a container. Or maybe a whole container. He did not know.

He remembered something about his right arm. He looked

at it. It was neatly bandaged from the mid-forearm to the mid-upper arm. Otherwise it was bare.

His other arm was bare too. So were his shoulders. Where was his shirt?

His trousers were gone too. So were his boots. So was his underwear. Beneath the blankets he was naked.

One of the times he had gone away someone must have undressed him.

Or perhaps he had been undressed before he was laid out.

This was highly improper. He should be wearing a brand-new suit.

Was it possible that he was not really dead?

He went away again.

This time he went all the way to Earth-present. And whom did he see but Miss Sands. She was in her office in the Chronology Department and he had just stepped into the room. Long had he yearned to apprise her of the unrequited love for her that burned in his breast, but he had never dared. But now he was a new Carpenter. Let her scorn his words if she must, but he would speak them.

He strode boldly across the room and confronted her across her neat desk. "Miss Sands," he said, "for ages poets have sung of love at first sight, only to be laughed at by their cynical peers. I wish to avow here and now that it is the cynics, not the poets, who are fools, for when you first swam into my visage, Miss Sands, love struck me senseless, as a bolt from the blue, and I have not been the same since. For months I have worshipped you from afar, not daring to reveal the way I feel, because I know my love is not returned. But it is far too rich a tapestry for me to defer any longer laying it at your feet, even though you do not want it, even though you will spurn it and regard it with disdain. So here and now I proffer it, Miss Sands, for you to do with as you please, to cast it into a corner, if such be your will, or to grind it contemptuously beneath your feet."

When next he came back, he found that he could sit up and no longer needed to lean against the propped-up back of his bier, and he found that the "bier" was made of folded blankets piled on a mattress of boughs. To the left of it and to the right were similar beds, and sitting next to his own bed on a folded blanket was the omnipresent angel with the chicken soup. The Princess of Greater Mars.

"Why are you crying, Pumpkin?" he asked, and she turned her face away. But then she turned it back, and there was the spoon again, and the throat-warming chicken soup.

Beside the Princess of Mars sat her brother, Skip. "Boy, you're going to be all right, Mr. Carpenter. Boy, you're going to be all right!"

Carpenter saw how clean their clothes were. It was as though they'd visited a laundromat. Surely there were no laundromats in Eridahn.

A container of milk appeared, this time without a straw. He sipped from it.

Looking to his left, he saw Sam. The reptivehicle was parked a considerable distance back from the vine-covered entrance. Its illusion field had been turned off, and Sam had neither tail nor legs. The built-in searchlight in his frill had been directed upward toward the lofty ceiling, and it was its reflected radiance that illuminated the nave.

Slanted sunlight was again streaming through the interstices. "Is it morning or afternoon?" Carpenter asked.

"Morning," Skip said.

"I can hear water running somewhere."

"It's an underground creek."

"I hope you kids aren't drinking its water."

"No. We know better than that. We use the water from Sam's tank for drinking. We just use the creek for washing in. Mr. Carpenter, we—we had to wash your clothes. They were all bloody."

"Where are they?"

"They're hanging back by the creek. I rigged up a clothes-line."

"Skip, where in the world are we?"

"We're where they quarried the limestone to make the ce-ment for the city. When they quarried it they made pillars to support the ceiling, and the place began looking so nice they went ahead and made it even nicer. They cut vaults into the ceiling, and when they kept quarrying farther and farther back they cut in a gallery and cut in a flight of stairs leading up to it. They kept quarrying beyond the gallery—the limestone's better there—and there are all sorts of tunnels—regular corridors—running way way back into the cliffs. The creek is an underground stream they discovered accidentally. It comes out of the wall beneath the gallery and then cuts back in where the stairs are."

"How'd you kids know there was such a place?"

"Deidre studied about it in the special school we go to."

"This cliff that we're in—it must be part of the same line of cliffs we camped next to."

"It is, but it's a long ways east of where we camped, and not far from the sea. The city's just south of us."

"How far south?"

"About five miles. The builders used a monorail to transport the limestone, but the towers that supported it have all fallen down."

"But the terrorists—the kidnappers—they must know about the quarry too."

"Probably they do, but when the colonists left they blew up the quarry's entrance—over there where all those big chunks of rock are—and from the outside it looks as though there's no place to get in."

"Why would they do a thing like that?"

"I guess they were just feeling mean."

"But you and Deidre found a place to get in anyway."

The boy nodded. "We were pretty desperate. After you fainted we had an awful time lifting you into Sam, and then we didn't know where to go. Then Deidre remembered the quarry, so we took a chance and headed here. She knew the colonists had blown up the entrance, but we figured there just might have been a hole left that would be big enough for Sam t pass through. We didn't find it till daylight, though, because of the vines that had grown across it."

The soupspoon touched Carpenter's lips. He swallowed its contents. Abruptly he sat up straighter on his bough bed. "You must have left tracks!"

"No, we didn't. I turned Sam's rear lights on and back-tracked him along the tracks he'd made over the plain. Then when I came to that creek we crossed when the kidnappers were bringing us to the city, I turned into it and drove Sam up it toward the cliffs. It's the same creek that goes through this chamber, and it comes out of the cliffs west of here. After we left it, Sam couldn't make any tracks because the ground was rocky. So the kidnappers could never track us here."

"You guys are pretty smart."

"We've got Sam's shield field focused on the entrance, so even if the kidnappers could track us, they wouldn't be able to get in."

"Shield fields can be shorted."

"They don't know enough to do anything like that."

The soupspoon again. Carpenter was surprised at how tired he was. After he swallowed the spoonful of soup he went away again.

When he came back, there was the Princess of Greater Mars again. It was as though she had never left. He saw that the vine-covered entrance was dark. "You must be tired, Pumpkin. Why don't you get some rest?"

"She sleeps when you do, Mr. Carpenter," Skip said from beside her. "Anyway, it's early yet. Eat some more soup. She just made it."

Sure enough, there was a bowl of soup on her lap and a spoon in her hand. This time he consumed the bowl's entire contents. Another container of milk appeared. "It's canned milk this time," Skip said. "The other milk got sour."

Carpenter took the container from Deidre's hand. She had mixed water with the milk, and it did not taste too bad. He realized he was using his right arm. It seemed as good as new. He looked at the neat white bandage. "How in the world did you kids stop the bleeding?"

"Deidre sewed the artery back together. There were needles and sutures and everything else she needed in Sam's cupboard. She's pretty good at stuff like that. She's studying it in school."

Carpenter stared at Deidre's face. "You sewed the *artery*, Pumpkin?"

She nodded. She was no longer crying, but her face was so mournful she might as well have been. "Well, it's nothing to feel sad about, Pumpkin."

She set the soup bowl on the floor and placed the spoon in it and got up and walked away.

"She's kind of touchy these days," Skip said.

"Why should she be touchy?"

"I don't know. I don't understand women."

"Neither do I," Carpenter said. "I guess I must have been an awful burden to you kids."

"No, Mr. Carpenter. Deidre and I are the burdens. If it weren't for you, we wouldn't even be alive. Or if we were, it wouldn't be for long."

"I'm not much help to you now, and I'll be of even less if I don't get up and start walking around. Get my clothes, Skip."

"Sure. Your boots are at the foot of the bed."

His legs were rubbery when, fully clothed, he got to his feet, and the nave—he still thought of the big quarried-out chamber as such—kept tilting. But he was determined, and, leaning on Skip's shoulder, he forced his legs to obey his wi!l. At length the nave straightened, and he saw the walls on either side and the gallery in the rear with the steps leading up to it. The gallery seemed to be more the work of sculptors than of quarriers. He could almost picture an art exhibit along its walls.

He did not try to walk all the way to the stairs, only far enough to see the underground stream. The reflected light was not bright enough for him to tell whether the water was turbid or clear. He had a hunch it was as pellucid as a mountain brook. He grinned at Skip's clothesline. It was a length of rope from Sam's storage compartment strung between two tree branches brought in from outside and jammed into cracks in the limestone floor. The cracks were probably a by-product of the explosion that had sealed the entrance. The same explosion had covered the floor with a thin layer of white dust.

He listened to the underground stream. He liked its soft-sweet sound. Then Skip helped him back to his bough bed. He saw no sign of Deidre. Probably she was inside Sam. His tiredness astonished him as he slumped down on the bed. He must have lost a great deal of blood while he was hammering on Hugh's jaw. He kicked off his boots. "Skip, maybe I should sleep for a while."

"Sure, Mr. Carpenter. And don't you worry about a thing. Deidre and I are here."

When he awoke he did not know how long he had slept. Probably not for very long, for the vine-covered entrance to the cathedral was still dark and he was certain he had not slept the clock around. Deidre was sitting beside his bed. He saw that her own bed was neatly made. Skip's bed was on the other side of his, and Carpenter saw that the boy was sound asleep beneath its topmost blanket.

Daylight could not be far away for there was a dawn chill in the big room. Deidre had no bowl of soup, no container of milk. Why was she sitting there in the cold? "Aren't you tired, Pumpkin?"

She shook her head.

The head of his bough bed had been lowered. He twisted around and found that the folded blankets that had propped it up had been pulled from beneath it. He knew it would be awhile before he could fall back to sleep and he did not feel like lying flat on his back, so he began trying to shove the blankets back in place. Deidre pushed his hands away and shoved them back herself. Then she sat back down again.

It was silent in the huge nave. It was a reassuring silence. The kids were with him and they were all right. Somehow he would have to get them back to Mars, but there was no need to worry about that at the moment. Anyway, if he could not get them back, he could always take them to Earth-future with him. What was important right now was that they were okay.

"Mr. Carpenter?"

He looked at Deidre. This was the first time she had ever spoken to him directly. He could not see her face clearly because Skip had turned Sam's searchlight down to a lower beam, but he could see it clearly enough to tell that she was crying.

Was she upset because of Hugh? he wondered. He found this hard to believe. Hugh had barely touched her. Then why was she upset? Why, almost every time he opened his eyes, did he find her crying beside his bed? "Pumpkin, there's no reason for you to cry."

"Yes, there is, Mr. Carpenter."

"I'm going to see to it that you kids are okay."

"I know you are, Mr. Carpenter. That's why I'm crying."

He did not know what to say.

"And," she went on, "I'm crying because I was so mean and wouldn't speak to you. You're the most wonderful person I've ever known. No one's ever been so nice to me as you

have, and no one's ever really cared before what happened to
me, and I wouldn't even speak to you because I'm a mean,
stuck-up princess, and I'm so sorry I just plain want to die!"

Carpenter reached out and touched her hair. She was in his
arms then, sobbing. "You didn't have to speak to me, Pumpkin.
I understood. And it didn't make me like you any less."

"You should hate me, Mr. Carpenter."

"How could anybody hate you?"

"Because I'm mean and stuck-up."

"I couldn't hate you even if I wanted to. If it wasn't for
you, I wouldn't even be alive. Not only that, you make the
best chicken soup I've ever tasted."

"It comes in cans—you know that, Mr. Carpenter. I didn't
even know it was chicken soup, whatever chicken soup is. All
I did was put water in and heated it."

"That's the trick," Carpenter said.

"Heating it?"

"Yes. The way it tastes depends on how it's cooked."

She looked up at him. "I think you're kidding me, Mr.
Carpenter."

"Maybe a little bit."

"Why do you call me 'pumpkin,' Mr. Carpenter? On Mars
pumpkins are unpleasant squashy fruits that grow in swamps
and midden marshes."

"Oh Earth, in my time, they grow in beautiful pumpkin
patches, and you can make delicious pies out of them. 'Pumpkin' is what a man calls a girl when he thinks the world of
her."

The smile that broke upon her face was like the sun coming
out after an April shower. "I—I like to have you call me that,
Mr. Carpenter."

"Right now, I know a certain 'pumpkin' who should be in
bed."

"My bed's right next to yours."

"I know."

"If you want anything, wake me up."

"You sleep tight, Pumpkin. I'm fine."

In the morning Carpenter found he was strong enough to
walk without assistance. The vine-covered entrance was gray

and he could hear the patter of raindrops. The kids were sound asleep. He walked over to Sam. The passenger-side door was open and he looked inside at the control panel. There were no red lights showing. Later on he would start the engine and let it charge the batteries for a while. Skip might already have done so, but it would not hurt to charge them some more.

He leaned against Sam's treads. With its illusion field off, the big reptivehicle looked something like an outsized bulldozer. He could have taken Edith, the big tyrannotank, and probably he would have if George Allen, who was supposed to accompany him, had not quit. Sam was more viable as a one-man reptivehicle.

He wished he could fix the kids breakfast, but he did not feel quite up to it. His right arm, though, was in fine shape. Deidre would be able to take the bandage off soon. He found it hard to believe she had sewed the severed artery together, although he knew it was true.

If it had not been for her he would probably have died. And if it had not been for Skip staunchly driving Sam through the night to the cliffs, the three of them would have fallen into the terrorists' hands again, and quite possibly by now all of them would be dead.

He felt his face. It was stubbled with at least a three-day growth of beard. He climbed inside Sam and went back into the cabin and got his shaving cream and razor out of the cupboard and shaved at the little sink. There was a showerhead on the wall and a drain on the floor and curtains that could be drawn to protect the rest of the cabin, but although the water gauge showed Sam's tank was more than half full he felt it would be unwise to waste any water. There was no need to in any case, since he could bathe in the creek.

He got a cake of soap and a big towel out of the cupboard, left the reptivehicle, and went back to the underground stream. The water looked cold. It *was* cold—startlingly cold. He had considerable difficulty because he did not want to get his hearrings and the bandage on his arm wet, but he managed. He toweled warmth back into his body and slipped back into his clothes. He felt like a million dollars.

Skip was up by this time. Deidre was still sound asleep.

"Gosh!" the boy exclaimed when he saw Carpenter. "You're walking around. And you *shaved*!"

"How long have we been here, Skip?"

"This is the fourth day."

"I guess it was high time then that I got up and started moving around."

"I'll wake up Deidre so she can fix breakfast."

"No. Let her sleep."

"I'll fix breakfast then, although I'm not much of a cook. I wish I could cook like Huxley."

"Huxley?"

Skip pointed to the gallery. "He's an old man who lives way back in the cliff."

"There's someone living back there and you didn't tell me?"

"I—I never really had a chance to, Mr. Carpenter."

"You kids shouldn't wander off like that and associate with someone you don't know!"

"Oh, but he's harmless, Mr. Carpenter. He was one of the colonists. When they went back, he stayed. He says he was fed up with Greater Mars and the whole planet for that matter, and never wants to go back there. He wants to meet you."

"Then why doesn't he show himself?"

"He's shy. I guess living all alone for so many years has made him afraid of people."

Deidre had awakened and was sitting up in her bough bed. She threw back the blanket that had covered her and slipped her feet into her boots. "Sleepyhead!" Skip said.

She got to her feet. Her autumn-aster eyes touched Carpenter's face. "Good morning, Mr. Carpenter."

"Morning, Pumpkin."

Skip was staring at his sister. "So you finally decided to climb down off your throne!"

"You shut up!" Deidre said.

"I was just going to fix breakfast."

"*I'll* fix breakfast." She looked at Carpenter. "I guess you wouldn't want chicken soup, would you, Mr. Carpenter?"

"I guess I've had enough chicken soup for a while. I was going to have coffee. And eggs."

"Oh. I—I don't know how to fix coffee. Or eggs."

"I'll settle for cocoa," Carpenter said. "I'll show you how to fix it. And how to fry eggs."

Skip was still staring at his sister. "Well, it was high time!"

"What do *you* want for breakfast?" Deidre asked.

"The same as Mr. Carpenter." Skip looked at Carpenter. "I just don't understand my sister."

"Women are mysterious," Carpenter said.

Deidre was walking toward the rear of the cathedral. "Where's she going, Skip?"

"She's going to wash up. I guess I'd better too."

"After breakfast I think we'll go visit Huxley."

"Do you think you can walk that far, Mr. Carpenter? It's quite a ways. He comes to the stream for water every day. Maybe we should wait."

"I think I can make it okay," Carpenter said. "At least I'll give it a try."

Maybe Huxley was harmless and maybe he was not. Harmless or not, he was a potential candidate for the fossil.

DEIDRE DID NOT LIKE the idea of Carpenter's walking so far so soon, and told him she thought he should wait at least until the next day before going to visit Huxley. He laughed and said he had taken a bath in the creek and that now he felt fine. She had a fit. "Mr. Carpenter, after losing so much blood you shouldn't have exposed yourself like that! It's a wonder you didn't freeze to death!"

"I—I guess I wasn't thinking very well, Pumpkin."

But he was still determined to visit Huxley, and at length she gave up arguing. Before they set out he took his raze pistol from Sam's door holster and slipped it into his belt. It was just like two kids, he thought, to make friends with someone about whom they knew nothing, although he suspected that Skip alone was the guilty party, since it was unlikely Deidre would have had much to do with a total stranger.

She and Skip led the way. Carpenter had self-doubts when

he started up the limestone stairway. Was he really strong enough to make the climb? The kids mounted it slowly, and presently Deidre dropped back to his side. He grinned at her. "I'm doing fine, Pumpkin."

But he was glad when they reached the gallery.

It was so meticulously sculpted that it brought to mind the gallery of an opera house. He had never been in an opera house, but he was certain this was the way a gallery in one would look. The corridor openings along the rear wall were like the entrances through which the members of the *haut monde* would pass to their posh seats.

He had upped the beam of Sam's searchlight before they set out, but very little of the light reached this far back in the cathedral. Perhaps if he could have seen better he would have been able to detect flaws, and the gallery would have lost its elegant aspect.

Skip turned into one of the corridors. He had taken one of the flashlights from the drawer beneath Sam's control panel and now he flicked it on. The corridor was quite wide. Deidre, who had remained at Carpenter's side, continued to do so. "We'll let Skip lead the way," she said.

"Don't you know it?"

"No. I never went with him when he visited Huxley. But I saw him the times he came for water."

The floor of the corridor slanted upward. At length Skip came to a Y and took the left branch. Deidre and Carpenter followed. The branch slanted upward too. Then Skip made a left turn into another corridor, then a right into another. The upward slant continued, and Carpenter was certain they were nearing the top of the cliff, a considerable distance back from its face.

Another left turn, another right. Carpenter tried to remember the route. He wished he was not so poor at directions. Presently he discerned a light up ahead—a tiny dot. As it grew larger it acquired the shape of a small square. Finally it was revealed for what it was: the open peephole of a door.

"Huxley," Skip shouted, "I'm here! I brought Mr. Carpenter and my sister."

He had halted just in front of the door. It was a steel door, Carpenter suspected, similar to the doors in the city. A face appeared beyond the peephole. Wrinkles, and a pair of dim blue eyes. A straggling of gray hair. Skip stood on tiptoe so his face would be visible through the hole. The door swung slowly inward, and the light from the room beyond showed it was steel, as Carpenter had suspected.

But he was far less interested in the door than in the old man who had opened it. Huxley no doubt had been small to begin with, and age had made him smaller yet. His hair was combed the way Einstein had combed, or had not combed, his. His caved-in cheeks indicated he had no teeth. His skin tone was gray. Only his dim blue eyes lent life to his face, and the impression was undermined by their emptiness. Carpenter remembered the bleakness of the terrorists' eyes. Maybe, years ago, Huxley's had been bleak too. He was wearing a tattered knee-length tunic that resembled the skin of a hadrosaur, and probably once had been, and grotesque shoes which had been carved from wood.

"Come in, come in," he said in a timorous voice. "I'm home."

"I brought Mr. Carpenter and my sister," Skip repeated.

"Fine. Fine."

Home was a large low-ceilinged room which had been quarried out of the limestone. In its center was a crude wooden table flanked by three crude wooden chairs. Upon the table an egg lantern emitted a mellow glow. In the wall opposite the door was a similar door. This one had a steel-meshed window that framed a sizable square of gray daylight. The wall on the left was tiered with wooden shelves which were filled with folder-like volumes. Arranged along the opposite wall were kitchen utilities: a stove, a crude wooden cupboard, and a metal tub. The tub was filled with dirty dishes. Between the cupboard and the stove was an archway that led to another room, or possibly a closet. There was a trapdoor in the ceiling. It was on tracks. Maybe it covered a skylight, steel-meshed like the window in the door. Carpenter was certain the room was just below ground level. A series of steps, or possibly a ramp, probably led down to the outside door.

The cathedral, which had seemed so secure, had had a back door all along. But it was unlikely Huxley ever left it open. "Welcome to my humble quarters," he said to Carpenter.

A better adjective would have been unkempt. The floor was an inch thick with grime and the wall above the stove was multicolored with stains. The room smelled of ancient garbage. Maybe Huxley smelled too, but the garbage smell was so intense it was hard to tell.

"Deidre," Skip said, "you've another pair of hearrings. Give them to Huxley so he can understand Mr. Carpenter."

Deidre did so. After Huxley affixed them to his ears, Carpenter said, "You've lived here ever since the colonists left?"

"Yes. Ever since." Huxley pointed to the table and chairs. "Please have a seat, sir."

He led the way to the table. Carpenter chose a chair that looked slightly cleaner than the others. Skip sat down in another, and Huxley took the one next to Carpenter. Deidre was forced to remain standing. She did not seem to mind.

"Skip told me you're from the future," Huxley said.

"The far future."

"He said seventy-four million years. I didn't believe him. I do now. I can see you're not a Martian, and it's unlikely the Ku would seed this planet much before that length of time."

"How can you see I'm not a Martian?"

"It's quite obvious, even though you're physically identical to us."

"You implied the Ku are going to seed Earth. With humans like yourself. The age I'm from has a diversity of different races with markedly different histories. They're all basically the same, but they're of different colors and have superficially different physical characteristics. You and the kids are like my particular race, but surely there must be other races on Mars besides yours."

"There are. But there are no physical differences between them and I don't even know what you mean by different colors."

"Then the Ku must have used only one type of seed. If they're going to populate Earth, they're going to need a variety of types."

"I think the seeding of Mars was an initial experiment. Naturally the Ku will go on to more complex endeavors."

"But why did they seed Mars with humans right off the bat and start an evolutionary chain on Earth that eventually resulted in reptiles?"

"I don't know. But I don't think they expected the chain to result in reptiles. That's why they're here."

"You've seen them?"

"Oh, yes. Several times."

"What do they look like?"

"They're geometric. I think they're going to destroy the reptiles. At least some of them."

It was as though the old man had looked into the future. But Carpenter was far from being convinced that the Ku would be responsible for the extinction of the dinosaurs. He was far from being convinced, in fact, that the Ku existed.

He pointed to the volumes on the shelves. "Reading material?"

"Yes. I read a great deal. I used to hunt till I ran out of charges for my rifle, and now reading is about all I have to do. The volumes you're looking at constituted the best material of the Rimmon library. I brought them here after the colonists left. I brought a host of other items as well: a stove, a dishpan, eating utensils, tools, knives for butchering, a lifetime supply of rations, a lantern and a lifetime supply of fuel cells, and steel doors for my new home. It took me days to drag everything here. The doors were the worst. Twice I was attacked by dinosaurs and nearly lost my life."

"Why didn't you stay in the city?"

"Because it reminded me of Mars. Mostly because of its architecture. I wanted to forget Mars. When we came to Earth we brought Mars with us. I was the Chief Assistant to Rimmon's Construction Engineer, but I had nothing to do with the architectural design."

"Did Skip tell you about the kidnappers?"

"Yes. I'm doubly glad now that I didn't remain in the city."

"The kidnappers—I call them terrorists—hate the Greater Mars Establishment. You said you wanted to forget Mars. Do you hate the Establishment too?"

"Yes, but only passively. Once I was a very small part of it. Naturally you know nothing about our planet, Mr. Carpenter—our planet, that is, as it is now—except what the two children may have told you. There are five major nations. Greater Mars, geographically, is the smallest, but it's the most technologically advanced, and yet we stubbornly maintain a

silly, almost nonfunctional monarchy. The monarchy's icing
on a cake compounded of power-seekers and wheeler-dealers
and, of course, the inevitable hoi polloi. The double dealing's
the worst. I could almost use the term double-double dealing.
You can't rise by reason of merit to positions of even minor
power. You have to cheat your way up and keep ingratiating
yourself with the powers-that-be. Desentimentalization, to which
every Martian of every country is submitted at the age of thirteen, is a farce insofar as true efficiency is concerned. Did
Skip tell you about desentimentalization, Mr. Carpenter?"

Carpenter nodded.

"Well, it works just fine up to a point. When a desentimentalized person makes a decision he never makes it under
the influence of love, affection, or compassion. Nevertheless,
the decision is seldom objective. Desentimentalization simply
makes more room for greed. The island continent of Greater
Mars, excluding the Royal Family, which already has more
money than it knows what to do with, is populated by two
kinds of people—those who've double dealed and ingratiated
themselves into high-paying positions and those who are desperately trying to. If you're inefficient in the art of sycophancy,
as I was, you're doomed to remain forever in the ranks of the
hoi polloi. But I was lucky. More by accident than by design
I was made Chief Assistant to Rimmon's Construction Engineer. I was on the verge of being made Construction Engineer
of the second city Greater Mars planned to build in the highlands, and then the project was abandoned. When I was robbed
of this opportunity to prove myself and to obtain the salary one
of my merit deserved, my bitterness overcame me. I resolved
to have nothing further to do with the island country of my
birth, or the planet of which it's a part."

"Greater Mars is an island?" Carpenter asked.

"Yes. A huge island. I've no idea what Mars is like in your
day, but at this point in time its northern hemisphere consists
of a great ocean which surrounds a small ice-covered continent
at the pole. The island of Greater Mars is in the eastern hemisphere, situated not far north of the vast landmass that covers
almost the entire southern half of the planet."

Elysium, Carpenter thought. Huxley was talking about Elysium. Earth geologists in the future had theorized that there

might have been such an ocean and that Elysium might have been an island. "If Greater Mars is the place I'm thinking of," he said, "there are still pyramids there. One of our space vehicles photographed them. Three-sided ones. A four-sided rectangular one."

"The Ku built them, long before our time. Of a strange material we've never been able to analyze and for reasons we've never been able to imagine. I'm not surprised that they're still standing. As you may have noticed from Rimmon, they've had a marked effect on our architecture. I wonder what else remains of modern-day Mars."

For Deidre's and Skip's sakes, Carpenter avoided painting a picture of Mars' future face. Instead he stayed on the subject of the pyramids. "On Earth in my country," he said, "we're building a huge obelisk in one of our western deserts to commemorate the completion of another century of American civilization. It's called the God Bless America Obelisk. It was begun twelve years ago and is scheduled for completion by the turn of the century. It's far higher than anything we've ever built—far higher than anything any race on Earth has ever built—but the pyramids on Mars dwarf it."

"You seem to have reached the acme of your civilization," Huxley said, "the way we Greater Martians at this point in time have apparently reached the acme of ours. Whether we have or haven't, we've climbed just about as high on the ladder as we're ever going to get. Our paleontologists estimate that the Ku seeded the planet about twenty-two hundred years ago. Right after the last ice age. Now another ice age is on the way."

"I'm sure it's far enough in the future not to affect your way of life."

"It certainly won't affect *my* way of life, Mr. Carpenter."

"I was thinking of the prince and the princess."

"The prince and the princess?"

"Skip and Deidre. Deidre is next in line for the throne. Didn't you know?"

Huxley had stood up. His face was ashen. He bowed to Deidre. "Your Highness, my apologies." He bowed to Skip. "Your Highness, why didn't you say?"

"I guess I never thought to."

Huxley shuffled around the table, dragging his chair. "Please, Your Highness, be seated," he said to Deidre.

Deidre shook her head. Then she looked at Carpenter. "Mr. Carpenter, are you all right?"

The room had just done a somersault before Carpenter's eyes. Now it steadied itself. "I was just a little dizzy for a moment. I'm okay now."

"You are not! Skip, help me. We've got to get him back to bed!"

To show her how strong he was, Carpenter stood up before she and Skip reached his side. She did not buy his bravado. "I told you it was too far for you to walk!"

She seized one of his arms and Skip the other. "It was nice talking to you, Huxley," Carpenter said over his shoulder.

"Come again, Mr. Carpenter. When you're feeling better." Huxley bowed again to Deidre and Skip.

The corridors maintained an even keel. Perhaps this was because Skip kept the beam of the flashlight directed at the floor and Carpenter was unable to see the walls. He was glad when they reached the stairway, glad at last to see his bough bed and to drop down upon it. "Skip, get another blanket out of Sam," he heard Deidre say. And then he heard no more.

_____Chapter

_____9

CHICKEN SOUP AGAIN. And the angel sitting at his bedside.

He did not know how long he had slept, but the darkness of the entrance indicated it was night, and Skip, sound asleep in his bed, lent the impression it might even be the middle of the night. The beam of Sam's searchlight had been turned down.

"Pumpkin, you should be in bed."

"Eat some soup, Mr. Carpenter. I just made it."

His bed had been propped up again. "How'd you know I was going to wake up?"

"I woke you up. You need nourishment more than sleep. The soup, Mr. Carpenter."

He swallowed the contents of the spoon that she was holding before his lips. "Here, I can feed myself."

"No, you can't, Mr. Carpenter, because I'm not going to let you."

"You're bossy tonight."

"I don't mean to be bossy, Mr. Carpenter. But you had me worried sick. Here, drink some milk."

He obeyed. It was watered-down canned milk. "Pumpkin, how did Huxley know I'm not a Martian? The terrorists knew right away too. And so did you kids. How can everybody tell so quick?"

"Because of your face. It isn't hard the way Martians' faces are. And your eyes are different too. They're gentle instead of bleak."

"So are yours."

"I'm only a kid. And besides, I haven't been desentimentalized yet."

He thought of the terrorists. "Do all grownup Martians have faces like Kate and Floyd and Fred and Hugh?"

"Most of their faces aren't *that* hard. But they're hard enough. And their eyes are just as bleak."

"Huxley's face isn't hard. And his eyes are empty."

"That's because he's old. But the hardness is still there underneath. Eat some more soup, Mr. Carpenter."

"After I'm through eating I want you to go straight to bed."

"I will, Mr. Carpenter. Here, drink some more milk."

"Yes, ma'am."

In the morning he felt fine and she let him walk around a little. He said he could stand some bacon and eggs for breakfast and told her where the bacon was and how to fry it. She fixed cocoa too and brought him a tray. The tray was the breadboard from Sam's cupboard, but it sufficed. She held it steady while he ate.

Skip sat down on the other side of his bed. "Did you like Huxley, Mr. Carpenter?"

"He seems harmless enough."

"He came for water this morning. He looked over this way and I thought he was going to pay us a visit, but he didn't. He went back up the stairs."

"Why don't you turn Sam on and let him idle for a while so his batteries'll be in good shape."

"All right. I've been doing that off and on all along, Mr. Carpenter. Didn't I tell you I'm a mechanical genius?"

"Well, you don't have to keep bragging about it!" Deidre said.

"I'm not bragging!"

"Yes, you are!"

"The rule for the day," Carpenter said, "is no family quarrels."

The tempest in a teapot subsided, and Skip headed for Sam.

Since Deidre insisted that he stay in bed except for a brief walk every now and then, Carpenter spent most of the day dozing off at intervals and thinking of the kids between times. Deidre removed the bandage from his arm and replaced it with a much smaller one. The cut was healing nicely. He told her she made him think of Florence Nightingale, and when she asked who Florence Nightingale was he told her she had been Earth's first real nurse. Deidre said that in Greater Mars all girls were taught nursing and medicine. This got him to thinking that perhaps the unpleasant picture Huxley had painted of his native land might have been a caricature. Greed was anything but a unique motivating factor, and it was difficult to believe that Greater Mars had any more double dealers than the good old U.S.A. would have 74,051,622 years from now. As a matter of fact, despite its mandatory desentimentalization program, the Greater Mars civilization might be a good civilization to be a part of, particularly if you happened to be key members of its Royal Family.

This brought him back to Square One: how to get the kids back to Mars. Huxley's mention of a forthcoming ice age had given him pause for a moment, but he didn't take it into consideration because all his life he had been hearing about a forthcoming ice age on Earth and regarded such catastrophes as inevitable future phenomena people could do nothing about. An ideal answer to his problem would be to jump Sam back to the moment Kate and Floyd and Fred had been drinking on the fourth floor of the safe house and he had been fighting Hugh on the third. It would be a cinch then to enter the ship and radio Greater Mars. But too much time had gone by, and if Sam were to jump back that far now, his batteries would burn out before he got there, or, if they did not, burn out on the way back, leaving Carpenter and the kids with an inoperable reptivehicle in the very shadow of the terrorists' ship.

The only viable answer would be to sneak Sam close enough to the ship so it could be kept under surveillance and blend him in with his surroundings and then simply wait till the terrorists left the ship unguarded. It would be a long wait, because the terrorists knew that the radio represented the kids' only chance of ever being rescued and they would watch over it the way a mother hen watched over her chicks; but eventually there would be a slip-up. Maybe Hugh would get drunk again and leave his post. Or maybe fall asleep. In the latter case, Carpenter would have to sneak on board to find out, and this would be a risky undertaking. He would take it in his stride if and when the moment came, but the important thing right now was to get the project underway as soon as he was back on his feet, for the terrorists might decide to abandon the kids and settle for the ransom, which their confederate on Mars must have collected by this time, and take off for their home planet.

Deidre served him chicken soup and milk for lunch. Chicken soup was starting to come out of his ears. Also, he was sick of lying in bed. He had what he thought was a brilliant idea. "Why don't you let me fix the evening meal, Pumpkin? It's not fair, your doing all the cooking."

"I *like* to cook."

"Well, even though you like to, you must be getting kind of sick of it. What I'll do is get started early and fix something special and—"

"Mr. Carpenter, you're trying to trick me to let you get out of bed!"

"But I'm feeling fine. I—"

"Tomorrow you'll be feeling finer yet. Then you can get out of bed and do anything you want. But meanwhile I'm going to do the cooking!"

Well, anyway, it had seemed like a brilliant idea. But all was not lost. "In the freezer compartment of the refrigerator, Pumpkin, you should find some almost flat square boxes with pictures of food on them. They're what we in Earth-future call TV dinners. Ordinarily I hate them, but I think that tonight one would taste pretty good. If there are any, bring two or three of them out with different pictures on them."

She brought out a Macaroni and cheese, a Fried Chicken, and a Salisbury Steak and Potatoes. He pointed to the Salisbury Steak and Potatoes carton. "I'll have that one."

"I will too," Skip said from beside her.

"Are there two of them, Pumpkin?"

"Three. I'll have one too."

He read the instructions to her and she said she would remember them, and that evening they had TV dinners seventy-four million and some odd thousand years before TV would be invented. Deidre sat on one side of Carpenter's bed with her tray and Skip sat on the other side with his. It was almost as famous an occasion as the Marshmallow Roast, and this caused him to think of all the lonely miles that lay between Earth and Mars, and presently he found himself thinking of a slender princess with buttercup-color hair ascending a flight of golden steps to a golden throne, her face stone-hard and every last wisp of gentleness gone from her eyes, and he saw Skip, tall and grownup, his face as hard as Floyd's, standing among the members of the royalty who had shown up in all their finery for the accession, and he wished, wished with all his might, that he could in good conscience take the two kids to Earth-future with him, and knew in utter desolation that he could not.

He did not sleep well that night, perhaps because he had slept half the day. He kept twisting and turning in his bed. Finally he opened his eyes and sat up, and whom did he see sitting on a folded blanket beside his bed but the angel, also known as the Princess of Greater Mars.

Had she brought more chicken soup? More milk? No, she had neither. She was just sitting there alone in the night, her rumpled bough bed behind her.

"Can't you sleep either, Mr. Carpenter?"

"No. You shouldn't be sitting there, Pumpkin, you should be in bed. It's cold."

"I kept thinking about the fix Skip and I are in and worrying about what we're going to do, and it kept me awake. And then I saw that you were having trouble sleeping too."

"You let me do the worrying. I'm going to get you kids back to Mars somehow."

A silence. Then: "I also kept thinking about Miss Sands. About what you said about her not loving you."

"The Princess of Greater Mars has big ears."

"I couldn't help but hear when you were telling Skip about her when we were camped at the cliff. I was only pretending to be asleep, but I didn't mean to eavesdrop."

"Then you must have also heard me tell him that sometimes in Earth-future when a man falls in love with a girl she doesn't always fall in love back. That's the way it is with me and Miss Sands."

"I don't believe that for one minute, Mr. Carpenter. I'll bet she's keeping her love a secret the way you're keeping yours."

"Pumpkin, she won't even look at me."

"I'll bet she looks at you all the time when you're not looking back. *I* know how girls are, Mr. Carpenter. But you should never talk to her the way you did in your sleep. She might think you're kind of weird."

He remembered the dream in which he had entered Miss Sands's office and avowed his love. Obviously he must have spoken aloud. "I think Miss Sands already thinks I'm weird."

"She does not! Honestly, Mr. Carpenter, you make me mad sometimes! You can hardly expect her to fall all over you if you don't even talk to her! Why, I'll bet if you told her you loved her, she'd throw herself into your arms!"

"I don't think so, Pumpkin."

"You just try it next time you're with her and see!"

"I'll give it some thought. Meanwhile, I think both of us should try to get some sleep."

She leaned quickly forward and kissed him on the cheek. Was it the dim light that made her autumn-aster eyes so deeply blue? "Any girl would," she whispered. Then she slipped beneath the blanket of her bough bed.

He awoke to sunlight slanting through the interstices of the vine-covered entrance. The rain was over and gone. He got up quietly so as not to awaken the kids and slipped his feet into his boots. He shaved in Sam's cabin, then fixed breakfast.

Pancakes and sausage. A pot of cocoa. "Come and get it, you guys!" he called from the passenger-side door.

They ate in the cabin. As there were only two chairs, Skip had to sit on the edge of the bunk. His eyes grew big when he bit into a sausage link, bigger still when he put a large, syrup-smothered piece of pancake into his mouth. Deidre ate daintily, but when Carpenter asked who wanted seconds she did not say no.

To prove to her how strong he was, he insisted on doing the dishes. While he was doing them, Skip, who had gone outside, came to the passenger-side door and said that Huxley, when he had come for water, had said he had something important to tell Carpenter and would appreciate it if he would pay him another visit. Carpenter looked at Deidre, who was drying a plate. "Well, I guess it will be okay, Mr. Carpenter. But Skip and I are going with you."

Skip let Carpenter lead the way. After they reached the gallery he turned into the correct corridor, and when they came to the Y he took the left branch. But there were many side corridors to choose from, and he was not certain which one he should turn left into. Sure enough, he chose the wrong one, and Skip said it was the next one instead. Carpenter made the correction. Then it was necessary to make a right turn, a left, and finally a right. There were fewer side corridors now, and he found the way without further difficulty, and at length the dot of Huxley's peephole showed in the distance.

Huxley had slid the trapdoor aside. Morning sunlight filled the room. The place looked far dirtier in daylight than it had in the light of the lantern. The old man bowed to Deidre and Skip. He had found another chair somewhere and had placed it at the table with the others. He bowed again to Deidre. "Please sit down, Your Highness."

It was evident that unless she complied Huxley would remain standing. She perched as close to the edge of the seat as she could without falling off. Carpenter and Skip also sat down. Huxley seated himself in the remaining chair, across the table from Carpenter. "During your previous visit, Mr. Carpenter," he said, "I made mention of the fact that on Mars another ice age is on the way."

Carpenter nodded. Was this why Huxley had wanted him

to pay another visit? So he could talk about a theoretical ice age?

"Because of the eccentricity of its orbit and its extreme axial tilt, which ranges from fourteen to thirty-five degrees," Huxley went on, "Mars is a sitting duck for ice ages. One end of its orbit lies thirty million miles closer to the sun than the other, and sometimes when the planet's closest to the sun it's tilted so that its northern hemisphere is farthest away from the sun. At the opposite end of its orbit, when summer should reach the northern hemisphere, the planet's so far from the sun that summer doesn't fully materialize. During such phases, the ice at the North Pole doesn't undergo a normal melting process. Over a time period of about twenty-four thousand years, the situation is reversed, and the southern hemisphere is similarly affected. But in between these two climatic extremes there's a period during which the two hemispheres receive the same amount of sunlight. Then the ice around the polar caps is melted in a normal manner, water vapor is absorbed by the atmosphere, and the climate grows warmer. These ideal interglacial periods last close to three thousand years and must have been recurring throughout the relatively recent history of the planet. The Ku took advantage of the present period, for reasons known only to them, and seeded the planet with human and various other life forms. . . . You don't seem particularly surprised by the extreme variation of the Martian climate, Mr. Carpenter. I wonder if in your day and age a Martian ice age might be in effect."

Without thinking, Carpenter said, "You described a huge ocean to me when I was here before. There's no sign of one now. And when the planet's closest to the sun, its northern hemisphere's tilted away."

Dedire touched his shoulder. "Isn't there any *life* there, Mr. Carpenter?"

"We don't know, Pumpkin," he said quickly. "We've only photographed the planet with orbiters from a height that wouldn't indicate whether there's life or not and made a few simple experiments with telemetric landers. There could be life there, there could even be a subterranean civilization." He carefully refrained from mentioning that the atmosphere of Mars-future was mostly carbon dioxide and too thin to permit water to flow.

"But the Mars of my day is over seventy-four million years in the future, so it certainly isn't anything you or Skip need to worry about."

"Definitely not, Princess," Huxley said. "And the Mars of eight hundred years from now—which, as you no doubt know, is when our scientists have predicted the next ice age will begin—definitely isn't anything you or your brother need to worry about either. And you can believe that by the time anybody really *does* have to worry about it, spaceships will have been built capable of transporting the entire Greater Mars civilization to the planet of another star." Huxley returned his eyes to Carpenter. "I wanted you to be thoroughly familiar with the problem, Mr. Carpenter, and for you to understand that the coming ice age is so remote in human terms that it doesn't have any bearing on your dilemma."

"My dilemma?"

"On whether you should take the princess and the prince back to your future with you, or whether you should try to get them back to Mars."

"I'm afraid I never took your ice age into consideration."

"I was afraid you might have. That it might affect your thinking. Your dilemma is a tricky one. You know as well as I do that a princess and a prince can't be set down willy-nilly in just any society, and while your speech and manner indicate your particular society can't be radically different from that of Greater Mars, it has to be different in certain ways, and even if it weren't, you couldn't accord two members of royalty the way of life they've always taken for granted. The point is, they simply don't belong in Earth-future; they belong on the planet where they were born. Moreover, the princess is destined someday to ascend the throne of Greater Mars, and by taking her to Earth-future you would be robbing her of her birthright.

"But if you decide they should be returned to Mars, your only course of action will be to try to outwit the kidnappers and contact the Space Navy by using the kidnappers' radio, and this is a hazardous course indeed. So it's certainly not a dilemma that lends itself to an easy solution.

"When a man decides to become a recluse, he doesn't, unless he's feeble-minded, cut himself off irrevocably from his own kind. He makes certain his place of retirement—his cave, if you like—is close enough to civilization so that if something goes wrong or if he changes his mind, he can go back to where he came from. And if his place of retirement is remote from civilization, he makes certain he has a conveyance capable of covering the intervening distance. He leaves himself an option, and it's the option that makes his self-ostracism endurable. When he goes to bed at night and when he gets up in the morning, he does so with the knowledge that any time he really wants to he can return to the society he exiled himself from.

"As the Chief Assistant to Rimmon's Construction Engineer, I was provided with a ground car and, more importantly, with a private spacecraft in which I could journey back to Mars whenever there were holidays or whenever business matters made such a journey necessary. There's a small spaceport in the center of Rimmon where important officials such as myself kept their small craft. During exodus, I lifted off in mine with the ostensible intention of returning to Mars. But I didn't return. Instead, I orbited Earth several times and landed the ship at night in a gully beyond the cliffs. I'd already found this quarried-out section where we're sitting now. I've never used the ship since, but it's still there. Right at my back door. It's my option. As spacecraft go, it's a very small affair and lacks an interplanetary radio, but it can accommodate two adults—or one adult and two children. It hasn't the velocity of larger spacecraft, but with Mars and Earth in their present positions it's capable of making the journey between the two planets in less than seven days. Its cation drive is sealed, so no deterioration can have taken place. I inspected the antimass reactor yesterday. It's in perfect condition. What I propose to do, Mr. Carpenter, is to relieve you of your dilemma. I will take the princess and the prince back to Mars."

_____**Chapter**

_____10

IT WAS QUIET in the cathedral for all the rest of
the day. It was a time of waiting. The kids had no clothes or
anything else to pack, so there was nothing to preoccupy them
on this score. At noon Deidre prepared a light lunch. It was
singularly uninspired: cocoa and vacuum-packed sandwiches.
Neither she nor Skip seemed hungry. Carpenter had no appetite
whatsoever. He was certain the kids were lost in thoughts of
Greater Mars.

Take-off time had been set for 7:00 P.M., Carpenter's time.
Huxley did not have a clock and told time by the sun. He said
he would come for the kids. Carpenter kept looking into the
driver's compartment at the clock on Sam's control panel to
see how much time had gone by. He missed his watch. Huxley
had said he would need the whole day to pack the provisions
for the trip because the ship's limited storage space mandated
his taking only the most essential food items. Carpenter had

offered to furnish food from Sam's larder, but Huxley had said no, that he was too accustomed to a Martian diet and still had half a roomful of the rations he had collected in the city after the colonists' departure. When Carpenter had told him the food could not possibly have kept for the length of time Huxley had been living in his cave, Huxley had said that food, when properly vacuum-packed, would keep forever, and that on Mars vacuum-packing was an art.

The old man never intended to return to Earth. His reward, he had said, for taking the princess and the prince back to Mars should make him a superrich Martian, and there would be no reason for a superrich Martian to sulk for the rest of his life in a cave on Earth.

He had been quite frank about his motive. "I was born poor. Now I can die rich." Perhaps too frank.

The gully in which his spacecraft stood was less than a quarter of a mile from his hermitage. The ship was perched on delicate steel jacks and was no more than thirty feet high. In the beginning the old man had kept its prow camouflaged with tree limbs, which he had cut fresh weekly. Now this was no longer necessary, for the branches of the trees on the gully's banks had grown far enough out from their trunks to hide the ship. Skip had inspected its antimass reactor and found nothing wrong with it. He had not been able to inspect the drive, but since it was sealed it could not have rusted, so there was no valid reason why its parts should not be in working order.

Carpenter had inspected the module. It provided just enough space for an adult and two children to sit and just enough extra space for them to move about.

There was no reason in the world why Deidre and Skip could not go back to Mars.

That afternoon while Carpenter was taking apart the bough beds and folding the blankets, Deidre said, "I guess that now, Mr. Carpenter, you can return to 1998."

"No, I'm going to snoop around a little first, Pumpkin. I was sent back to find the origin of a fossil. NAPS won't like it if I come back with no concrete information at all."

"Are you going to tell them about Skip and me?"

"I sure am."

"They won't believe you found a prince and princess from Mars way back here in your past."

"Maybe they won't. But I'm going to tell them anyway. They'll have to believe something, though, when they see all the pictures of you and Skip that Sam took. I'm going to commandeer the best ones of you for myself, and frame them and put them on my mantel. Well, no, not my mantel, because I don't have one, but on the shelf beside my radio."

She was silent. He suspected she was thinking of the huge palace she would soon be living in again and all the servants who would be at her beck and call. She would forget about the marshmallows in no time at all. He swallowed. "I think that someday you'll make a marvelous queen, Pumpkin."

She turned away without a word and walked back to the rear of the nave, where the creek was. Puzzled, he stared after her. She sat down at the creek's bank and hunched up her knees and rested her arms on them.

He resumed folding blankets.

The trouble was, he knew nothing about Huxley except what Huxley had told him, and Huxley might not have been telling the truth.

Moreover, Huxley was an old man. His age was at least the equivalent of seventy-five Earth years. Conceivably it might be the equivalent of a hundred Earth years, since people on Mars might not age as rapidly as people in Earth-future would. But seventy-five or a hundred, he was nearing the end of his life.

Suppose he should reach the end of it midway between Earth and Mars?

Skip would have to take over the controls then. Probably he would be up to the task. But Skip was no more than nine years old!

But the real question was not Huxley's longevity but his trustworthiness. He had been living in a limestone cave for almost half a century. What had he been thinking about all that time? What notions, logical and illogical, had been born in his mind?

In how many various ways had his mental evolution differed from that of gregarious men?

* * *

"I cleaned Sam all up inside, Mr. Carpenter," Skip said. "He's all set now for you to go looking for whoever turned into a fossil."

"Thanks, Skip. Sam thanks you too."

He walked over to Sam and looked through the doorway at the clock: 1:56.

Living in a limestone cave for almost fifty years, and then one day, going to the creek for water, the old man had seen two kids, a big alien machine, and a man sleeping on a bough bed.

One of the kids made friends with him. He was not particularly impressed when he learned that the kid and his sister had been kidnapped, because he did not know yet that they were the Prince and Princess of Greater Mars. He did not find out who they really were till he met Carpenter, and Carpenter told him.

He had already told Carpenter that he hated the Greater Mars Establishment. He hated it passively, he had said. Passively, hell! Carpenter thought. Huxley must hate it with his bones. Otherwise he would not have chosen to take up residence in a cave millions and millions of miles from its sycophantic doorstep.

A princess and a prince. Overlords of the Establishment. Superficial overlords, perhaps, but overlords just the same.

The icing on the Establishment cake.

Why would an old man with but a handful of years left want to be rich?

Deidre got a roll of gauze bandage and a pair of scissors from Sam's cupboard and came over to where Carpenter was sitting on a chunk of fallen limestone near the entrance. "I think I should put a fresh bandage on your arm, Mr. Carpenter. There won't be anybody to bandage it for you till you get back to the future."

He watched her deft fingers unwind the old bandage and apply the new. He wanted to tell her again that she made him think of Florence Nightingale, but he remembered how she had walked away when he had said what a marvelous queen she would be and he was afraid of somehow offending her again, and so he said nothing.

He went over to Sam again and looked at the clock: 2:59.

Living in a cave the seasons round, year in, year out, for decades, with nothing but a batch of books to keep him company. Sitting there reading, remembering.

Remembering, perhaps, how he had been shuffled to one side time and time again when certain jobs he had wanted had come open, how he had been snubbed by people slightly higher on the ladder than he was; recalling, perhaps, the big tax bite that had come out of his wretched wages and visualizing the posh palace where the superrich overlords lived. Remembering how he had finally obtained a job commensurate with his abilities, how at last the appointment of Construction Engineer had been dangled before his eyes and then jerked away.

Remembering, resenting. Hating.

Hating the powers-that-be.

The wolf crawling out now and then from the lamb's clothing and skulking about the stone-walled room.

Discovering one day that the Princess and Prince of Greater Mars had strayed into its den.

Deidre fixed TV dinners for supper and made cocoa. The TV dinners were Macaroni and Cheese. "That's swell cocoa, Pumpkin," Carpenter said, sipping from his cup.

To his amazement, a tear ran down her cheek.

He saw them step into the module of the ship. He saw Huxley step in after them. He saw the lock close and the ship take off.

Fifty million miles...

It was six thirty by Sam's clock.

Deidre and Skip were sitting in Sam's passenger-side doorway. Their eyes were far away.

No doubt they were thinking of the palace and all the royal privileges that would soon be theirs again.

Carpenter, who had climbed past them and gone into the cabin for a glass of water, left by the other door.

A marshmallow on a stick was a poor substitute for an imperial scepter.

He went over to the vine-covered entrance and looked through the interstices at the late Cretaceous day. Live oaks grew just down the rocky slope from the cliff. They had long shadows. Birds with teeth flitted among their branches. A struthiomime was braced on its tail beneath one of them, nibbling on the lower leaves. The late-afternoon sky was a deep blue. The fresh air, cleansed of its humidity by the rain, actually sparkled. In the distance to his right he could discern the mountains. They were new upon the face of the Earth. He heard the faraway half scream—half roar of a theropod. The live oaks hid the plain. He pictured it in his mind, with its laurel and its sassafras, and its dwarf magnolias in bloom. Lovely Eridahn.

They were his kids, not Huxley's. So maybe they were the Princess and Prince of Greater Mars. He had found them. They were his. And if anything should happen to them he would die.

It was almost seven o'clock. Huxley descended the limestone stairs to the floor of the nave. Carpenter walked over and stood next to Sam. Deidre and Skip climbed down from the doorway and stood beside him. Huxley walked across the floor, his wooden shoes going *clunk-clunk-clunk-clunk*. He bowed to Deidre and Skip. "I believe it should be almost time to depart, Your Highnesses. My ship awaits your command."

"I've been thinking," Carpenter said. He turned toward Deidre and Skip. "I know how badly you want to go home, I know how you must miss the palace, and how you must miss your parents too, although you've never said so. I know how you must feel." He turned toward Huxley. "I know they'll probably hate me, but I just don't know enough about you to entrust them to your care." He looked at the kids again. "I'm sorry, but I just can't let you go."

He was astonished when they threw their arms around him and Deidre jumped up and kissed his cheek.

Chapter

11

CARPENTER FOUND THAT the boughs used for the beds had dried out sufficiently to be used for firewood. He sorted out the smallest ones, and Skip, guessing his intention, began building a small campfire.

"Pumpkin, see if there's another bag of marshmallows in Sam's cupboard."

"There is! There is!"

Tiny flames began to skip merrily from twig to twig, and the little pile of branches Skip had built up ignited. He had already sharpened a stick with a paring knife taken from Sam's cupboard. Deidre, with a similar knife, was sharpening another. Carpenter said, "Let's wait till the flames die down."

"Do you think Huxley was mad, Mr. Carpenter?" Skip asked.

"He probably was."

"He sure looked like he was, the way he walked away. I

guess it never entered his head you wouldn't be glad to get rid
of us."

Deidre had sharpened a second stick. She handed it to Carpenter. "I'll go make some cocoa."

"Later on," Carpenter said, "we're going to have a meeting."

Since the fire was a small one, the flames died down fast.
Deidre brought out the cocoa and three cups, and she and Skip
and Carpenter sat down by the fire. Presently the atmosphere
of the Cretaceous cathedral was introduced to the aroma of
roasting marshmallows.

The bag didn't last long.

Carpenter wished he could remember the words to some of
the songs he used to know, but he could not. The kids sang
one of their own. Its melody was delicate and moving and
made him think of the green hills and fields and the blue
canallike rivers he had seen in the mural in the safe house, but
the lyrics were about a fisherman who had caught his foot in
his net and lost all his fish. It was a lovely song just the same,
and he wished there were time to sing others, but there was
business to be attended to.

"I guess," Carpenter said, finishing his cocoa, "that both of
you know what the meeting is going to be about."

Deidre and Skip nodded.

"Although I couldn't let you go with Huxley, the point he
made is valid. Both of you belong on Mars."

Two more solemn nods.

"So somehow I've got to get into the kidnappers' ship and
radio the Space Navy. I think you said, Skip, that they can
make it here in a little less than five days."

"Deidre can figure out exactly how long it would take them,
Mr. Carpenter."

"There's no need for that just yet. The important thing right
now is to figure out how to get into the ship. That'll have to
be done when it's unguarded. If we were to jump Sam back
to various points within his jumping range, we might hit a
moment when whoever happened to be on guard temporarily
deserted his post. Then I could get on board. But the odds
against that happening just by luck are pretty steep, and—"

"But, Mr. Carpenter," Deidre interrupted, "even if you could

get on board unnoticed, you wouldn't know how to operate
the radio."

"You kids can tell me how."

"I think we should go with you."

"The trick is to get you back to Mars, not to have you wind
up in the kidnappers' hands again."

"But what good will it do us if *you* wind up in their hands,
Mr. Carpenter?" Skip asked.

"I won't."

"It seems to me," Deidre said, "that ever since you rescued
us from that big dinosaur you've been taking risks because of
us. I think *we* should take some."

"There'll be no risk to speak of if we do it right, Pumpkin.
What I was going to say was that our best bet will be for us
to park Sam close enough to the ship so that we can keep it
under surveillance, and adjust his illusion field so he blends
into the scenery. Then we'll simply wait till one of the kidnappers deserts his post. Eventually one will."

"Maybe we should wait a couple of weeks before we even
begin the surveillance," Deidre said. "By then they'll have
given up trying to find us and won't even bother to guard the
ship."

"I think we should wait even longer than that," Skip said.
"Just to make sure."

"I think you guys are trying to con me."

"No, we're not, Mr. Carpenter."

"Not much you're not. The point is, we can't afford to wait.
Sam still has plenty of food left, but it won't last forever, and
the kidnappers may give up any minute and leave."

"Maybe they've left already!" Deidre said.

"Maybe they have, but I don't think so. We'll start our
surveillance tomorrow. And that being the case, I think all of
us should get a good night's sleep."

"I've still got some cocoa left," Skip said.

"So have I," said Deidre.

"All I've got to say is that I know a certain prince and
princess who'd better drink their cocoa fast."

He had the kids sleep in the cabin. There would be little
point in reassembling the bough beds just for one night and he

had burned some of the boughs in the fire, but his real reason
for changing the sleeping arrangements had to do with Huxley.
The old man certainly lacked the aspect of a formidable foe,
but someone who had been living in a cave for almost fifty
years and who had just had a potential fortune snatched from
his grasp should not be taken lightly.

Deidre let Skip have the bunk and made a blanket-bed for
herself on the floor. After Carpenter turned off the cabin light
he extended Sam's shield field far enough back so that it included the reptivehicle. There was just enough space for him
to make a blanket bed at the foot of the nylon boarding ladder.
He dimmed Sam's searchlight, called good night to the kids,
kicked off his boots and lay down. He had been carrying his
raze pistol in his belt. He removed it and laid it on the floor
within easy reach. He felt a bit foolish taking such elaborate
precautions, but he knew what money meant in Earth-future,
and Huxley's discourse had revealed it meant the same thing
in Mars-present.

The light reflected from the lofty ceiling was far from bright
enough to bother his eyes; nevertheless, sleep was a long time
coming, and when at last it arrived it was sporadic, providing
him with hiatuses in which to think. His thoughts were second
thoughts. Maybe he had made a mistake in not letting Huxley
take the kids. Maybe he had acted more out of loneliness than
from concern for their well-being. Maybe the real reason he
had not let Huxley take them was that he had wanted someone
to keep him company besides Sam.

The light *did* bother his eyes. It was so bright, in fact, that
it had awakened him out of a deep sleep. He opened his eyes.
The light was positively dazzling. And, incredibly, it had descended from the ceiling and coalesced into a long, gleaming
blade. And now the blade itself was descending.

He rolled to one side. The big butcher knife cut deeply into
the blankets. Huxley raised it and swung it downward again,
but Carpenter had rolled onto the lower section of Sam's treads
and the blade hit their upper section with a bell-like clang. The
impact ripped the knife's handle from Huxley's grasp, and the
knife clattered across the floor. Huxley, a barefoot tatterde-
malion who looked as though he had fallen out of a dream,
turned and ran.

Deidre appeared in the doorway. "Mr. Carpenter, what's wrong?" Then she saw Huxley. He was halfway to the stairs, his bare feet flap-flapping on the floor. She saw the knife. "He—he tried to kill you!"

Carpenter had got to his feet. Skip joined Deidre in the doorway. "Skip, the flashlight," Carpenter said. "I'm going after him."

Skip got it from the control-panel drawer and handed it to him. Panning the floor with the light, Carpenter spotted the three-strand copper wire Huxley had used to short out the field. He picked it up and tossed it to Skip. "Turn the field back on and close the door. Don't either of you kids come out till I get back."

Huxley was halfway up the stairs by this time. Carpenter picked up his pistol, slipped his feet into his boots and pounded after him. When he reached the gallery, Huxley had disappeared. He singled out the corridor the old man must have taken and turned into it. He heard the distant *flap-flap* of bare feet. When he reached the Y he took the left branch. *Flap-flap-flap-flap.* The sound was more distant now Was Huxley losing him? Maybe the acoustics varied. What was he going to do to the old man when he caught up to him? Beat him up? Hardly. But he would tell him a thing or two and make it clear that if he ever tried to get the kids again, it would be his last try.

The *flap-flap-flap-flap* died out altogether. Huxley must have turned into another corridor. Assuming that he was heading toward his hermitage, and it was unlikely he would be heading anywhere else, he must have turned left. It was up to Carpenter to find the correct corridor. Would he fail as he had failed before? The place seemed like a labyrinth. He selected a corridor, turned into it, stopped and listened. He heard nothing except the sound of his own breathing. He shone the light ahead. He saw no sign of Huxley. He directed the light toward the floor. The dust was undisturbed.

He stepped back into the original corridor. The next left-hand corridor had to be the correct one. He stepped into it, stopped and listened. Silence. He shone the light on the floor. The dust showed footprints—many of them. Relieved, he ran ahead. By this time the old man must have made the next turn.

It was a right turn, Carpenter remembered. This time he found the correct corridor without trouble. He now had two more turns to make, one to the left and one to the right. He found the left-hand corridor easily and pounded along it till he reached the final one that led straight to the hermitage. But he did not see the dot of Huxley's peephole at its far end; instead he saw the rectangular light of the entire doorway.

He was breathing hard by this time. It had been uphill all the way. He moved slowly toward the lighted doorway, his raze pistol in his hand. Huxley had said he had run out of charges for his rifle. This was probably true, or he would have used the rifle on Carpenter instead of a butcher knife. He had left the knife behind him when he had run away, but Carpenter was certain he had other such knives, and perhaps he was lying in wait beyond the doorway, another blade raised for a lethal downswing.

There was only one way to find out. Carpenter edged into the lantern-lit room. But Huxley did not confront him. Chaos did.

A chaos of books.

There was a big gap in one of the volume-lined shelves, and the volumes were lying all over the floor. A trail of them led to the outside door, which was open. It was easy to figure out the new scenario. News of the whereabouts of the princess and prince would not bring Huxley as big a pile of money as bringing them back would, nor make him a big-league hero, but it would still bring him a small fortune and make him a minor-league hero. He could write off his attack on Carpenter by characterizing him as an unscrupulous villain from whom he had tried to free the kids and who had conned them into believing he was their friend. Deidre and Skip would try to correct the story when the Space Navy brought them back, but the mere fact that Huxley had made their rescue possible would discredit whatever they said.

He had grabbed as many of his beloved books as he could; now their weight did not matter. Carpenter followed their trail across the room and through the outside doorway and up a short series of steps. The trail ended on the starlit plateau, but he knew where the ship was. However, the last thing in the world he wanted to do was to stop Huxley, and so he paused

in the starlight and waited. At length the little ship lifted sound-
lessly into the sky. With it went his dilemma. All he had to
do was wait in the cathedral with the kids till the Space Navy
arrived. Once one of its ships had landed he would build a big
bonfire outside the cathedral's entrance so the rescuers could
easily find their way to his and the kids' hideout; then the
rescuers could take Deidre and Skip to Mars.

His worries would be over. Just like that.

He swallowed. He wished he had a cigarette, although he
had not smoked for five years.

The little ship was high in the Cretaceous sky by then, and
its drive came on, giving it a starlike wake. Such a starlike
wake! It expanded before Carpenter's eyes. It became a nova,
bright and blinding, only it was not a nova nor even a wake
anymore: It was the ship and Huxley and his books.

Carpenter stared at the blazing funeral pyre till it finally
faded away. He had made the right decision—but for the wrong
reason.

He knew one thing for sure: The petrified human skeleton
NAPS' field workers would dig up in A.D. 1998 would not be
Huxley's.

_____Chapter

_____12

DAWN DISCOVERED CARPENTER and the kids and Sam far out on the plain.

Carpenter had been tempted to leave the cathedral far earlier than they had so they could creep up on the terrorists' ship during predawn darkness, but he knew he would not be able to find his way without recourse to Sam's searchlight, and the light would have given them away.

Before they left he had slipped outside and made a nocturnal reconnaissance of the immediate area. He had seen no sign of the terrorists, but he had to make certain they had not set up an ambush.

It was clear they had no idea where he and the kids had been hiding.

The first rays of the sun disintegrated Dawn's pink dress and sent her scampering westward. The curtain of the day having risen, the plain had now become an open stage. The stands of trees patterning the morning scene were too few and far apart for Carpenter's liking, but he knew there was no way entirely to avoid exposure while semicircling the city to where the terrorists' ship was located.

He maintained a wide semicircle and kept scanning the sky. But he saw no pseudopteranodons. To the west he discerned a herd of ceratopsians. Was it the same herd Sam had become a temporary member of a week ago?

Deidre and Skip were sitting with him in the driver's seat and they had seen the herd too. "Look at all the Sams!" Skip said.

"Look," Deidre said, pointing. "There's the tree that big fat dinosaur chased us up!"

Carpenter glanced at the tree. It might be the same ginkgo he had found the kids sitting in, but there were many ginkgoes on the plain and there was no way to tell for certain.

Skip had climbed back into the cabin. "Want a bottle of pop, Mr. Carpenter?"

Carpenter shook his head. "I'll have one," Deidre said.

Skip opened two bottles, handed her one, and climbed back up front with his. "Say, look at that crazy tree over there, Mr. Carpenter!"

It was indeed a crazy tree. It had a tail and a big head. And pointed teeth. It was sunning itself in the slanted morning sunlight.

Mr. *Tyrannosaurus rex.*

"Well, I knew I'd meet up with you sooner or later, old buddy," Carpenter said.

The tyrannosaur was not only sunning itself, it was watching Sam. It thought Sam was for real, and no doubt it was ravenous for a ceratopsian steak.

Its yard-long mouth was partially open, and the six-inch teeth it had developed especially for biting into the thick hides of ceratopsians awaited row upon row to tear into breakfast. It had a long red tongue.

It seemed to be grinning.

Carpenter slowed Sam to a crawl.

The kids had forgotten their pop and were staring at this culmination of reptilian evolution. Balanced on its huge hind legs, the creature stood at least twenty feet high. From the tip of its nose to the end of its gargantuan tail it measured at least forty-five feet. Its diminutive forelegs had two taloned fingers each, ideal for picking up teacups. It was dark gray in color and had a dirty, crawly hide.

A big glob of saliva ran out of the corner of its mouth and dropped with an almost audible plop to the ground. It roared. Or screamed. It was difficult to tell which. "Let's get out of here!" Skip whispered.

The tyrannosaur advanced. The ground trembled beneath its tread. "We're done for now," Deidre breathed.

"You kids stop worrying," Carpenter said. "It's no match for Sam."

Nevertheless, he wished he could use Sam's howitzers, just in case. But he could not without alerting the terrorists.

The tyrannosaur had now shut out the sunlight, and Sam was engulfed in its awesome shadow. The great head poised for a downward plunge. Carpenter locked one tread and made a quick right turn. This provided the tyrannosaur with a shot at Sam's tail. The trouble was, Sam did not really have a tail. The big jaws just missed the shield field and came together like two taxicabs colliding on Fifth Avenue. Then the tyrannosaur really let out a roar.

"He's—he's mad now," Skip said.

Carpenter spun Sam around till he was facing his adversary again. The tyrannosaur still thought Sam was a ceratopsian and expected him to charge the way a ceratopsian should. It would then step to one side and lower its massive head and sink its teeth into Sam's back. But Sam had other "thoughts" and, instead of charging, continued to back away. This further enraged the tyrannosaur, and instead of waiting any longer for the charge, it charged itself. Immediately Carpenter reversed Sam's direction, and when the tyrannosaur had all its weight on its right foot, banged Sam's shoulder into its left hind leg.

Only by swinging its tail wildly did the tyrannosaur avoid toppling.

Screaming now, it opened its jaws to full width, exhibiting each and every one of its six-inch teeth. The screams blasted its breath through Sam's vents, and his interior began smelling like a New York City street during a garbagemen's strike. Now the tyrannosaur bore down on him again, all memory of what had happened the last time gone from its mind. This time Carpenter barreled Sam into its right leg as it was about to lift it from the ground. Desperately, the tyrannosaur tried to execute a pirouette. It had as much success as an elephant trying to tap-dance. It flailed its mammoth tail in vain. To the three occupants of the reptivehicle it was like a tree falling. Carpenter maneuvered Sam so it would not fall on them. Down, down, down went the eight-ton mass of flesh. It took two small trees with it. CRAAAAAAASH! CRAAAAAAASH! KAROOOOOOOMPF!

Flat on its back, the tyrannosaur kicked furiously with its hind legs and flopped its tail back and forth till at length it rolled over onto its belly. But it was still in a dire predicament. When it was standing up the weight of its tail counteracted the weight of its huge head, allowing it to balance itself on its hind legs, but now that it was face down on the ground the tail was not quite heavy enough for the balance to be restored. So it went to work with its delicate forelegs, endeavoring to push its chest high enough above the ground to relevel the teeter-totter of its head and tail. When it had almost succeeded, Carpenter drove Sam over to the scene of operations and nudged its shoulder with Sam's snout, and down it went again, this time with a modified KAROOOOOOOMPF!

Deidre and Skip were laughing. "Tip him over again, Mr. Carpenter," Skip said when the tyrannosaur again managed to roll onto its belly.

"No. We've already given him a bad enough time. We'd better be on our way."

"Won't he follow us?" Deidre asked.

"I don't think so. Sam doesn't smell like a ceratopsian and he doesn't leave tracks like one. Anyway, he could easily outrun our friend over there. Do you kids think we're past the city?"

"Quite a ways past it," Skip said.

"Maybe, though, we'd better stay on a southeast course for a while longer."

"If we went directly east we'd wind up where the ship is."

"Maybe we can sneak up to it better from the south. We'll give it a try." Carpenter set Sam off across the plain.

"Pretty soon we'll see the sea," Deidre said.

The sea disconcerted Carpenter when, about half an hour later, Sam breasted a rise and it came into view. It disconcerted him because in A.D. 1998 it would not be there. Actually it was not a great deal different from seas of the future, although it was much, much shallower, of course, and its coastline was a tree-tangled swamp. But it was as blue as the Pacific and seemed to be as vast.

What disconcerted him far more than the sea was the huge pattern that presently took shape in the sky on a direct line with Sam's slanted windshield:

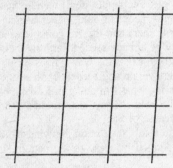

"It's the Ku," Deidre whispered.

The pattern lay directly in the path of the sun, which was now a third of the way up the eastern slope of the sky. The sun's brightness should have obscured it but did not. Its lines were blacker than the sun was bright.

"Those are only crisscrossed lines, Pumpkin. Why do you say it's the Ku?"

"That's the way the Ku look."

"Have you ever seen them?"

"No, but I've talked to people who have. But even though I've never seen them, I've seen the pyramids, and on each pyramid there are crisscrossed lines like we're seeing now."

"It's the Ku all right," Skip said.

"Wouldn't it be more apt to be a Ku spaceship?"

"It could be," Deidre said. "Even the scientists of Greater Mars aren't sure whether it's actually the Ku who appear in the sky and who are pictured on the pyramids, or whether it's their spaceships."

"You kids don't seem scared."

"We're not," Skip said. "The Ku never pay any attention to people."

"The pattern up there seems interested in us."

"I think they're interested in Sam," Deidre said. "He's an anachronism."

"So am I."

"But it's like Skip says, Mr. Carpenter. They never pay any attention to people. People just don't seem to matter to them."

"I should think people would matter a great deal if they seeded Mars with them and they're going to seed Earth."

"I think they've already seeded Earth in one sense. I don't think time for them exists the way it does for us."

"Well, if they've already seeded Earth in the future, they must be wondering what I'm doing in Eridahn now."

"No," Deidre said. "They just wouldn't care. If they're curious, it's because of Sam."

"Look," Skip said, "they're on the windshield now!"

Carpenter returned his gaze to the pattern. It *was* on the windshield.

He was reminded of a story by Poe which he had read in school. The hero, during a reign of cholera in New York, had spent a fortnight with a relative in the latter's cottage on the Hudson. Reading one afternoon by an open window that afforded a view of a hill, he had raised his eyes from the page and seen a grotesque monster crawling down the hillside. Ultimately the "monster" had proved to be an insect of the genus *Sphinx*, about a sixteenth of an inch in length, which was descending a filament of web that a spider had left hanging from the window sash.

Had the pattern been on Sam's windshield all along?

If so, it could not be much larger than Poe's bug.

The temperature inside Sam was dropping rapidly. Carpenter checked the thermostat. It was set at seventy degrees. The temperature continued to drop. He could see his breath. He could see the kids' breath. And he saw that now they were scared.

Deidre moved closer to him. Skip moved closer to Deidre. "I—I think they're exploring Sam," Deidre whispered.

"How, Pumpkin?"

"I—I don't know."

"Look!" Skip cried, pointing at the sky. "The kidnappers!"

Raising his eyes, Carpenter saw three "pteranodons." No, four. They were flying southward high above the littoral. He tried to throw Sam into gear so he could drive him beneath the branches of a nearby willow, only to find the engine was no longer running. He saw that the ignition was still on.

The terrorists had not spotted the reptivehicle yet, apparently, for the pteranodons' flight continued. Finally the four dark shapes faded from sight. But Carpenter knew they would be back.

"Maybe they saw the Ku," he said. "Maybe that's what brought them out."

Deidre shook her head. "If they'd seen the Ku they'd have stayed in the city. The sky's a good place to stay out of when the Ku are in it. I think they're just plain looking for us."

Carpenter thought so too.

He returned his gaze to the pattern. Was it really a group of alien beings, or was it only one alien being? Or was it, as he had suggested, a spaceship?

If it was a spaceship and originally had been in the sky, how could it have reduced itself to a minute fraction of its former size and moved instantaneously to Sam's windshield?

What it looked like was an awry tick-tack-toe diagram someone had drawn on the glass. Whatever it was, it had only two dimensions.

But maybe when they exhibited themselves or their ships, the Ku did so only two dimensionally. Or maybe humans were incapable of perceiving them or their ships in more than two dimensions.

Conceivably four dimensions might be involved.

He wondered what the pattern would look like from the outside. He tried to open the driver-side door. He was not particularly surprised when it would not budge.

He knew without trying it that the passenger-side door would not budge either.

Sitting with the two kids, he experienced a sense of cold

indifference. It was like the indifference one felt sometimes when looking up at the stars. He knew suddenly what Deidre had meant when she said that people did not seem to matter to the Ku. And he understood how a race of people could be aware of their creators and not worship them.

"Are the Ku seen very often on Mars?" he asked.

"People see them all the time," Skip said.

"They've been seeing them for generations," Deidre added. "The Ku are part of our history."

"If they're going to seed Earth, they should be a part of ours. But they aren't."

"Maybe the Ku have lost interest in Earth by A.D. 1998 and don't show themselves any more," Deidre said. "Or maybe they've gone somewhere else in the galaxy. But I'll bet there are traces of them in your culture."

Was it possible, he wondered, that the tick-tack-toe diagram had resulted from an archetypal memory? "Maybe you're right, Pumpkin."

He looked at the pattern again. It was no longer as distinct as it had been. And the temperature inside Sam was rising. The kids were looking at the pattern too. "It's going away," Skip said.

The crisscrossed lines had become filamentous, and the temperature continued to rise. Abruptly Sam's engine resumed running and the pattern vanished.

Carpenter had not thought to look at Sam's clock when the pattern first appeared on the windshield, but the position of the sun told him that the pattern had been there for a long time. It did not *seem* like a long time, but maybe during the Ku's presence, time had doubled its pace. Or perhaps the Ku ship, if it had been a ship, had effected an instability factor that had disturbed time's normal flow with regard to his perceptions, and perhaps Deidre's and Skip's as well.

"The kidnappers!" the boy cried. "They're back!"

"And they've seen Sam!" cried Deidre.

Three pteranodons were already swooping toward the reptivehicle. Quickly Carpenter drove it beneath the branches of the nearby willow, and the three craft rejoined the fourth one in the sky.

The *fourth* one?

Carpenter looked up through the interstices of the foliage and counted the craft. Yes, there were four of them.

The terrorists' ship had been left unguarded!

Deidre was looking at him. He saw that she too had made the deduction. Skip made it a second later. "They're so eager to find us they forgot about the ship. But it won't do us any good," he added, "because they can get there before we can."

"No, they can't," Carpenter said, feeding figures into the Llonka computer.

Deidre leaned forward. "Those are the same numbers as before, Mr. Carpenter."

"Right. It wouldn't be practicable to go back more than an hour. Put on your thinking cap, Pumpkin."

"828,464,280 times 4,692,438,921 is 3,887,518,032,130, 241,880."

Carpenter finished the computations and threw the jumpback switch. "Here we go again, you guys!"

Sam shimmered, there was a slight jar, and the sun back-tracked and the willow's shadow lengthened and the pteranodons vanished from the sky.

Chapter
13

THE TERRORISTS' SPACESHIP looked like a big metallic tree with three thin trunks. Its "foliage" consisted of a tangle of dead branches and withered leaves affixed to its prow.

The three trunks comprised the steel jacks on which it stood. They were slender and seemed very delicate, and Carpenter found it difficult to believe that they could sustain the ship's weight. Perhaps the steel mills of Greater Mars were several steps ahead of those of Earth-future.

Real trees stood in the ship's vicinity. Several ginkgoes, almost as tall as the ship was, a number of willows and some cycads. The level of the plain was lower here, and the ground was thick with sedges. There were numerous bogs. Carpenter surmised that the terrorists had chosen the spot because it afforded excellent concealment for the ship.

Deidre seemed to read his mind. Sam was on idle about

fifty feet from the ship, and she and Carpenter and Skip were still sitting in the driver's compartment. They knew the terrorists had already left because Carpenter had stopped on the way and waited till they had seen the pteranodons wing southward.

An open boat-bay lock near the ship's prow provided extra evidence of their departure.

Deidre said, "It's a good hiding place for the ship, but it was dumb of them to land it here with so many bogs around, especially because if the Space Navy ever guesses they're in Eridahn they can locate the ship with matter detectors. Not that they'd ever guess."

"Don't the terrorists have a hideout on Mars?"

"Yes. That's where Kirk is. He's their confederate."

"Why didn't they take you and Skip there instead of bringing you all the way to Earth?"

"Because Earth isn't really very far for a fast ship like that. It's a Space Navy reconnaissance ship they probably stole from the orbital yards. I'll bet the Navy hasn't even missed it!"

"The members of the Space Navy don't seem to be very smart."

"Oh, they're smart enough when they enlist, Mr. Carpenter, or before they go through the academy. But they're taught not to think—just to obey orders."

"They do everything by the numbers," Skip said.

"The silly part of the whole thing is," Deidre said, "is that we don't need a Space Navy. There hasn't been a war in a hundred years."

"You guys are lucky you're living on Mars."

"Are there wars in Earth-future, Mr. Carpenter?" Skip asked.

"We've had some big ones," Carpenter said. "Right now, though, we've managed to achieve a worldwide peace." He opened the driver's side door. "I'm going to get to the radio. We've lost half the hour we gained already."

"*We're* going to get to the radio," Deidre said.

"No. You kids wait in Sam and—"

"Mr. Carpenter, you can't possibly operate a Martian radio and you don't even know where it is, and even if you *did* know where it is and *could* operate it, how would you be able to speak to anybody on Mars unless they had hearrings on?"

"They'd put hearrings on."

"No, they wouldn't. They'd just think it was some nut who'd tuned in on the interplanetary band and tune you out."

"Anyway," Skip said, "what danger is there? How can the kidnappers bother us if they're not here?"

Carpenter looked at the ship. The entry lock was near the base, not far above one of the jacks. He could reach it by shinning up the jack. But what if he could not open it? He knew nothing of Martian mechanics.

He finally faced the fact that he could not do the job alone. He drove Sam beneath a willow and parked him so that his nose was pointed toward the nearest jack. It always paid to have an ace up your sleeve. "Okay, Pumpkin, okay, Skip—let's go."

They approached the ship, Carpenter in the lead. "Skip, do you think you can open the lock?"

"Easy, Mr. Carpenter."

He shinned up the jack and the lock opened to his touch. "It wasn't even secured, Mr. Carpenter."

Carpenter frowned. Things were proceeding too smoothly.

Skip lowered a flexible metal ladder. Carpenter ascended it first and Deidre followed. It was hotter inside the ship than without. The lights in the air-pressure chamber had been left on. Why? Skip opened the inner lock as easily as he had the outer and led the way into a corridor. The lights in the corridor had been left on too.

The boy was not altogether sure of himself. The corridor was circular, and he moved slowly along it. At wide intervals there were steel doors on either side. He opened one in the inner bulkhead and closed it. "The drive and antimass reactor chamber. We don't want to go there." Next he opened one of the doors in the outer bulkhead. "Look, Deidre—a secret stairway! Well, maybe it's not a secret one, but it's not the one they used when they brought us on board and took us off."

Deidre joined him in the doorway. Carpenter leaned over their heads. A spiral stairway led upward through a well comprised of smooth metal walls. The stairs were so narrow only one person could have ascended or descended at a time. "Maybe it's an emergency escape route, Skip."

"I'll bet it is! But we'd better go up the regular stairs, if I can find them."

They continued moving along the corridor, Skip still in the lead. They passed another door on the inner bulkhead, which he said also led to the drive and antimass reactor chamber. Then the corridor ended before a much wider door. "I think this must be it." He opened it, revealing an orthodox stairway. "This is the one they used when they brought us on board and took us off, Mr. Carpenter. It's the companionway. Come on."

He started up the stairs. Diagonal tubes of light illuminated them. Apparently the terrorists had left the lights on in the whole ship. Carpenter and Deidre followed. Carpenter was trying to keep track of the minutes that were going by. He could not, of course. But he was not really worried. Although they had lost much of the hour they had gained, there still should be plenty of time left to send the SOS. Once they had sent it, they would hightail it for Sam. He would keep Sam out of sight for the rest of the day, then head for the cathedral, where they would wait for the Space Navy to show up.

The first deck they came to was a green garden. Plants much like terrestrial ferns grew in well-watered troughs of mulch. Sunlamps inset in the bulkheads provided them with artificial sunlight.

The next deck comprised the galley and mess hall. It had a foul smell, the more noticeable because of the green smell of the deck below. Cartons were piled haphazardly about the big room. Cupboards were built into the bulkheads and a long, bolted-down table lined with bolted-down benches stretched almost from wall to wall. There was a filthy inset stove and an inset sink. Like the sink in the safe house and the tub in Huxley's hermitage, it was filled with dirty dishes. Didn't people do dishes on Mars?

The next deck was a big round room whose walls were the hull of the ship. It was empty except for rubbish scattered on the floor. "This used to be the crew's quarters when the ship was still part of the Navy," Deidre said. "I guess the kidnappers must have thrown out all the beds."

Skip pointed to a cylindrical column near the hull. "That must be the same stairway we saw below, Mr. Carpenter. It's even got a door in it. It's an emergency escape route, all right."

The deck they came to next must have comprised the officers' quarters. No doubt it was where the terrorists spent their time when they were in space. It consisted of a large rec room surrounded by a number of doors, all of them closed. There were six plush, bolted-down chairs arranged in a circle about a low pedestal in the room's exact center. On the pedestal rested what appeared to be a large ice cube. Carpenter did not need to ask the kids what it was. Although he had never before seen a Martian holo cube, he knew he was looking at one now.

Deidre pointed to one of the doors. "They kept us locked in there."

"They watched holo movies all the time," Skip said. "We could hear some of the words sometimes."

Blue movies probably. And the kids lying there, hungry and cold. Carpenter tried to hate the terrorists more than he did already. He discovered he could not.

The lower part of the pedestal had circular shelves filled with small spools which probably fed into the interior mechanism of the set. With so many movies to watch and with such comfortable chairs to lounge in, and, no doubt, with comfortable beds to sleep in, why, Carpenter wondered, had the terrorists chosen to take up residence in the safe house?

Maybe they looked on the safe house as Home Sweet Home.

The next deck looked like a huge computer room. There were panels everywhere with little lights on them, and switches and arrays of knobs, and tiers of screens. Carpenter had seen a similar room in Huxley's little ship, but naturally it had been much, much smaller and had failed to impress him. Skip had said it was the antimass reactor room. But this room was not only far larger, it was far more complex, and Carpenter was confused. "Why all the hardware," he said, "if the actual reactor's down below?"

"The reactor computer's incorporated with the ship's," Deidre said. "But of course it's still pretty big. It takes a lot of figuring to cancel out a planet's mass, and human intelligence just isn't up to it."

"I guess you have to be a genius to fly a Martian ship."

"You don't have to be a genius," Skip said. "All the pilot needs to know is which buttons to press in the control room."

He started up the companionway again. "The control room's two decks up yet. That's where the radio is."

The intervening deck was the pteranodon boat bay. A breeze from the plain, born in the mountains, flowed through the open lock. Near the lock the enclosed spiral stairway stood like a steel column. There was no inner lock, probably because the flyabouts were not space vehicles.

Several of them were stacked against one of the bulkheads. With their wings collapsed they looked like big leathery kites. The egg-shaped bombs they carried were packed into three steel-mesh containers which were secured to the deck. One was partly empty.

Carpenter walked over to the open lock. The kids joined him. The willow beneath which Sam was parked did not stand nearly as tall as the ship, and he could see the plain rolling away beyond its topmost branches, and, faraway, the young mountains which someday would be known as the Rockies. To his right, through gaps among the leaves and branches of a ginkgo, he glimpsed some of the pyramidal buildings of the city, and far beyond the buildings he could see snatches of the limestone cliffs. He looked to the south, straining his eyes for a sign of the pteranodons, but he knew that it was much too soon for them to appear. But he also knew that once the terrorists rearrived above the rise on which Sam stood and Sam did his vanishing act from beneath the willow, they would head straight for the ship.

Beside him, Deidre said, "It's such a beautiful place, Mr. Carpenter. I'm going to miss it when I get back to Mars."

"Mars must be beautiful too."

"Oh, it is. But not like this. When people live on a planet very long they rob it of something. In lots of ways they make it more beautiful, but in many ways they make it much less."

Carpenter thought of Earth-future. To think of Earth-future was to think primarily of highways and cities. Cloverleaves possessed a beauty of sorts when viewed from above, and cities seen from far away had a romantic aspect their interiors belied. But nothing man had ever built, or ever would, could touch the pristine loveliness of Eridahn.

It hurt him to think that soon he too would be leaving this

lovely land Time had tucked away, and he turned away from the lock. "I guess we'd better get to the control room, kids."

Again Skip led the way. Most of the control room was as incomprehensible to Carpenter as the antimass reactor and computer room had been. It occupied half the deck, and there were several doors in the bulkhead behind it. Two chairlike pads equipped with straps faced a maze of panels and screens and twinkling lights. To the extreme left and right of the chair-pads, inset in the hull, were two giant viewplates. Through one of them Carpenter could see the sea, and through the other, the plain.

Deidre and Skip sat down on the chair-pads, and Deidre reached toward a small hexagonal object attached to one of the panels. At this juncture one of the doors in the rear bulkhead opened, and Floyd, wearing a big, toothy grin and carrying a rifle, stepped into the room. Deidre and Skip, hearing his footsteps, twisted around in the chair-pads; their faces turned white. Floyd's grin transmuted to a big smile and he pointed the rifle at Carpenter. "Welcome aboard, old buddy."

_____**Chapter**

_____14

"I THOUGHT, PUMPKIN," Carpenter said, "that there were only four kidnappers."

"That *is* all there are, Mr. Carpenter. The fourth flyabout must have been a drone!"

Floyd, having no hearrings in his ears, had not understood Carpenter, but had guessed the nature of the remark from Deidre's answer. "We figured what you'd do if you saw four flyabouts," he said. "And we finally figured out something else. The only buddy you've got is a remote-control device. I kind of think it's that big buckle on your belt, but before you take off the belt, lay that little gun you've got tucked in it on the deck."

"Anything you say, Floyd." Carpenter laid the raze pistol on the deck and began unbuckling his belt. To Deidre and Skip he said, "You kids stay in those seats and strap yourselves in."

While unbuckling his belt, it was a simple matter to turn

the liaison ring with his thumb. He said to Deidre, "Pumpkin, if the ship were to fall on its side, would its impact with the ground set off any of those bombs in the boat bay or cause an explosion of any other kind? Answer me with a yes or a no."

"No."

"Skip, is the equipment on this deck secured tight enough to keep it from flying around as a result of such impact? A yes or a no."

"Yes."

"The seats—will they hold in place?"

"Yes."

"Do both you kids have yourselves strapped in tight?"

A dual "Yes."

"You quit talking to those kids and get that belt off!" Floyd shouted. He was hurriedly attaching hearrings to his ears.

Too late, old buddy, Carpenter thought, and pressed the X-shaped ram nodule on the ring.

Instantly from below came the roar of a Camins engine and the grind of treads. A blank look stultified the hardness of Floyd's face, and he ran over to the west viewplate and stared through it toward the ground. What he saw caused him to forget Carpenter altogether, and after throwing a switch beneath the plate that caused it to recede into the hull, he leaned through the aperture and aimed his rifle at the battering ram below. A split second later Sam made contact with the jack, the ship lurched, and Floyd, his rifle still in firing position, went flying through the aperture like a jet-propelled Darius Green.

C R A A A A A A A A A A C K! went the jack.

Carpenter dived for the seats and squeezed himself between them. "Hang on, you guys!"

The downward journey was slow at first but quickly picked up momentum. Then the momentum slowed, as Carpenter had hoped it would, as the ship crunched into the willow from beneath which Sam had begun his charge. Branches crackled, and the trunk, before it collapsed with a tremendous *crack*! twisted the ship partly around. But the ultimate impact was only modified. It tore Carpenter from between the seats and deposited him flat on his back on the interior of the grounded hull. Then somebody turned off the lights.

* * *

Somebody turned them back on again. He saw Deidre's face above his own. Her autumn-aster eyes were dark with anxiety. She had unbuttoned his plaid shirt and was patting his cheeks. He essayed a big grin that did not quite make the grade and took deep breaths of air to replace the wind the fall had knocked out of him. Then, gingerly, he got to his feet. Nothing seemed to be broken. The control room was intact too, but it looked strange because he was standing on one side of it instead of on the deck.

Deidre threw her arms around his waist. "Oh, Mr. Carpenter, you're always getting hurt because of us!"

He ruffled her buttercup-color hair. Then, in sudden alarm: "Where's Skip?" he asked.

Before she had a chance to answer, Skip climbed into the horizontal room by way of the horizontal stairway. He was carrying a small tank. "Mr. Carpenter!—you're okay!"

"He went after some oxygen for you," Deidre said. "But I guess you don't need it after all."

"No. I feel fine."

He did not, quite. He was still a little dazed. But he saw no point in saying so to the kids. He looked for his pistol but could not find it. Then he went over to the viewplate aperture, which was now positioned so that it could be used as a doorway, and stepped through it to the ground. The willow tree was a shambles. He looked beyond its smashed branches and broken trunk for Sam, but he was nowhere to be seen. Could the ship have fallen on him? Hardly. He must have been well beyond it when it toppled. Carpenter pressed the home nodule on the liaison ring and went looking for Floyd.

How quiet it was! The sauropods and ornithopods and theropods and ankylosaurs and ceratopsians for miles around, not to mention the lizards and the turtles and the frogs and the crocodilians and the insectivores and the various creatures of the sea, must have heard the ship fall and paused in their daily operations.

When he failed to find Floyd he thought at first that the terrorist might have survived the fall and was lying in wait for him in the sedges. Then he came to one of the bogs that infested the area and saw its soiled surface.

There was no sign of the rifle. Apparently Floyd had never let go of it.

Maybe if the NAPS field workers, when they dug up Floyd's petrified skeleton, would dig deeper, they would find his petrified gun.

As Carpenter stood staring at the bog, Sam trotted up to him and stopped a few feet away. He was a sad-looking reptivehicle. His illusion field was still on, so he still had legs and a tail, but the "unbreakable" windshield had shattered and most of the top of his head was gone. One of his horn-howitzers faced south and the other north, and there was a big dent in his snout.

Carpenter released him from remote control. He hoped NAPS would not take the repair bill out of his paycheck.

Deidre and Skip had come running over. He pointed to the bog, but they were more concerned about Sam than about the fate of Floyd. "Oh, Mr. Carpenter—he's ruined!" Skip cried.

"He can be fixed," Carpenter said, "and he's still operable." By now his mind had completely cleared. "Come on, you guys, let's send that SOS! Or did you send it already?"

"No, not yet," Skip said.

"Well, let's get with it then. While you're sending it, I'll look for my pistol."

They were a considerable distance from the fallen ship. They hurried back to it. When they reached the viewplate aperture, Deidre glanced at the sky. She stiffened. "Mr. Carpenter—they're back!"

The sky had four mean little specks in it. "Run for Sam, kids—quick!"

They took off, and he followed. They easily outmatched his longer but far slower strides and climbed into the driver's compartment before he had covered half the distance. The specks had resolved themselves into pteranodons, and the pteranodons were already diving toward the ship. When the terrorists saw what had happened to it, they would blow him to smithereens. As though to provide them with a maximum opportunity to do so, he tripped over a small turtle that was crossing his path and sprawled on his face.

Regaining his feet, Carpenter saw that Deidre and Skip had

closed Sam's passenger-side door. An instant later the tricer-atank shimmered, then disappeared.

Almost at once the sedges began to flatten as though from a mighty wind. He felt the wind himself, and it was blowing downward. Then he saw the great ship settling slowly toward the plain. It was so huge it looked like an airborne Empire State Building.

As he stared at it, jacks extruded themselves from its base and it came to rest on a quarter of an acre of land. The jacks adjusted themselves till it stood perfectly straight on the plain, and a second later four rainbowlike beams of light shot forth from its steeple and the four pteranodons—the manned ones and the drone—went PFFFFFFFFFFFT! PFFFFFFFFFFFT! PFFFF-FFFFFFFT! PFFFFFFFFFFFT!

The street doors opened, a gangplank as wide as a Fifth Avenue sidewalk extended itself, and down it marched two columns of troops. Their uniforms were of an alien cut and dazzlingly white, and each man carried a silvery rifle.

The columns halted at the base of the gangplank and turned and faced each other. Perhaps five minutes passed. Perhaps ten. Maybe even a quarter of an hour. Then a tall man appeared in the big doorway. His uniform was so white it made those of the troops seem dingy, and a ladder of multicolored ribbons fell from his left shoulder all the way to his belt. Carpenter thought of the operetta *H.M.S. Pinafore*. Here, surely, was the Ruler of the Space Navy.

Whoever he was, he strutted down the gangplank, walked between the two columns, and stepped out into the open. He was carrying a twinkling stick that looked like a wand. He stared at Carpenter across an intervening expanse of dwarf magnolias and sedges. Carpenter was about to walk toward him when Sam popped into view in the exact spot he had vanished from. Black smoke was pouring through his broken windshield. His illusion field was no longer functioning and he looked like a combat tank that had barely made it back from a battlefield. His passenger-side door swung open, and Deidre and Skip jumped out in the midst of more smoke. Carpenter understood what they had done then and kissed the twentieth century good-bye.

They ran over to him. "Oh, Mr. Carpenter," Deidre cried,

"we didn't want to burn him out, we thought maybe he wouldn't, but jumping back far enough so we could radio for the Space Navy soon enough so they could send a ship here in time was the only way we could save you from the kidnappers' bombs!"

"But how in the world did you get on board the ship without their seeing you?"

"It was night, and we used the emergency escape stairs," Skip said. "It was easy."

"But you took a big chance."

"It wasn't really much of a chance at all," Deidre said, "because we knew we wouldn't be caught for the simple reason we wouldn't have been there if we had been."

"Hugh was on guard," Skip said. "We peeked into the officers' quarters, and he was sound asleep in one of the chairs. Deidre figured out exactly how soon a ship would have to get here to save you and we told them over the radio and we told them everything that had happened to us. Everything would have been just fine if the time machine hadn't broken down. I had to take it apart and fix it. I studied it when you were recovering from your wound, Mr. Carpenter. I got to know it upside down. I fixed it in no time at all. We—we thought the batteries would hold up, but the return trip was just a little bit too much for them."

"But even though they burned out," Deidre said, beaming, "no great harm was done, because now you can come to Mars with us, Mr. Carpenter."

"Just like that," Carpenter said.

"We'll get you a swell job in the palace," Skip said, "and—"

"I regret having to interrupt so quaint a colloquy," an austere voice said, "but military procedures dictate that all missions must be implemented as expeditiously as possible."

Turning, Carpenter got his first close-up of the face of the Ruler of the Space Navy. The hardness of the terrorists' faces had not disconcerted him because he had expected it, but in the present instance he had been taken unawares. He saw a stern forehead. a stern nose, a pair of stern cheekbones, two ledges of lips, and a stone chin. A veritable cliff of a face, with two mean little brown eyes looking out of two shadowy caves. Gazing beyond it to the faces of the rest of the landing party, he saw similar cold, abrupt countenances.

The Ruler of the Space Navy bowed to Deidre and then to Skip. He ignored Carpenter. "You have never met me, Your Highnesses, but I have often viewed you from afar. I am Horatio, Commander of the flagship *Starfast*. The concatenation of events ensuing your abduction, together with orders from my superiors to arrive on Earth exactly when you said I should, were relayed to me by Naval Communications, but I would appreciate it, Princess Deidre, if you will relate to me personally all that you and your brother have experienced since your arrival on Earth."

Deidre did so. Carpenter found himself blushing as she got deeper into her narrative, because most of it was about him. According to her, his exploits on behalf of her and Skip had been nothing short of heroic, and he emerged from the tale as a sort of Eridahn culture god. "So what we've got to do," she concluded, "is take him to Mars with us and give him the welcome he deserves and find a high-salaried position for him in the upper echelons of the Kingdom."

Horatio did not seem to be in the least impressed, but at least he had been made aware of Carpenter's existence. He fixed his eyes on Carpenter's face. They were like dirty little brown marbles. Casually he attached a pair of hearrings to his ears and then gave Carpenter a lofty nod.

Carpenter ground his teeth. Then he reminded himself that officers of the Martian Space Navy were probably members of a rigid caste system and had been desentimentilized as well. How then could Horatio see him other than as a clod? "She's right about your taking me to Mars with you," he said, "although I certainly don't expect a high-paying position. Any old job will do. As she said, my reptivehicle's no longer operative, and while there's a chance I could get to my entry point on foot and send a distress signal to the future, it's a pretty slim one."

Horatio somehow managed to look down on him even though he was not the least bit taller. "I have no orders to take you to Mars."

Deidre's autumn-aster eyes flashed. "Well, you have now! *I* order you to!"

"May I remind you, Princess Deidre, that although your putative authority by far exceeds my official authority, no one, not even you, Your Highness, has true authority till she or he is desentimentalized. Thus I have no recourse but to leave this Earthman, to whom you accord kudos and whom you describe in such sentimental terms, precisely where we found him. On the planet where he was born—or, more accurately, the planet where he will be born, if we are to believe what he's told you, over seventy-four million years in the future."

Deidre was beside herself. "You're the Commander of a Space Navy ship. So if you haven't got an order to take Mr. Carpenter with us, *make* one!"

"I'm sorry, Your Highness. The issuance of such an order is beyond the scope of my command."

"Then radio Greater Mars."

"With regard to so insignificant a matter? I dare not do so, Your Highness."

"Then I will!"

"That will be out of the question, Your Highness. Space Navy radio communications can be made only by ship's personnel and are limited solely to communications relative to official naval operations. Please move back on the plain a ways, Your Highness. And you also, Your Highness," Horatio said to Skip. "It's necessary for me to extirpate all traces of the kidnappers' ship, which the Navy has no further use for now that it's been violated by their unscrupulous use of it."

"You just don't want anybody to find out they stole it right out from under your noses!" Deidre said.

"Please, Your Highness," Horatio repeated, "step back."

Deidre took Carpenter's hand. "I guess we'd better do what he says, Mr. Carpenter. Come on, Skip. I don't think what he's going to do will hurt Sam."

After Carpenter and the kids and the landing party had moved back a dozen yards, Horatio raised his wand. It turned blue, then green. Then a rainbowlike beam flashed from the Empire State Building's "steeple" and struck the terrorists' ship and disintegrated it from stem to stern.

What could have been a smug smile created a brief quiver in Horatio's lip ledges. He beckoned to two of the members of the landing party. "Escort the princess and the prince on board the *Starfast* and see to it that they have quarters commensurate with their noble station."

"I'm not budging one inch," Deidre said, "till you agree to take Mr. Carpenter with us!"

Horatio lifted the little finger of his left hand, and the two men who had stepped forward gingerly seized Deidre and Skip and began "escorting" them forceably toward the ship. The kids fought to free themselves, but the escorts were big, strong men. Carpenter watched helplessly, aware that Horatio would like nothing better than to order his men to riddle him with their beam rifles.

The kids were now being pulled up the gangplank. "Why didn't you take us to Earth-future with you, Mr. Carpenter?" Deidre cried. "We wanted you to all along!"

"I wish I had, Pumpkin. I wish I had!"

"There's a can of chicken soup left that you can send back. Oh, Mr. Carpenter, I hope you make it okay!"

"Maybe you can fix Sam," Skip called. "Maybe you can get at least one of the batteries to work."

"I'll be all right, you guys. Don't you worry about me." Carpenter confronted Horatio. "The least you can do is leave me a rifle."

"I'm not permitted to dispense military equipment to unauthorized personnel."

"I didn't think you would be."

The kids were now in the Empire State Building's doorway. "Good-bye, you guys—I'll never forget you."

Deidre made a desperate effort to free herself from her escort. She almost succeeded. Carpenter saw her anguished face. "I love you, Mr. Carpenter!" she cried, just before she and Skip were pulled into the ship. "I'll love you for the rest of my life!"

He found he could not see very well, and he knew he had made a terrible mistake. The kids did not belong on Mars any more than he did.

With two lightning-quick movements of his left hand, Horatio jerked the hearrings from Carpenter's ears. Then he said something unintelligible to his men. They formed a canopy with their rifles; he marched through it, they fell in behind him in two straight columns, and the landing party reboarded the ship.

The street doors closed. The Empire State Building quivered, then lifted from the ground. Its landing jacks retracted. It hovered there in the morning light, a huge, grotesque building with two lonely kids imprisoned inside it. The plain cover bent beneath its mighty antimass thrust, then it leaped into the sky and became an evanescent daytime star.

Carpenter stared for a long while at where the star had been. He saw the faces of the two kids. But they were not the faces he had known before. Time had jumped ahead and the kids had grown up, and their faces were hard and unfeeling, and all the love that had once resided in their eyes and that had reached out to him and touched his heart was gone.

He lowered his eyes to the plain. *I love you, Mr. Carpenter! I'll love you for the rest of my life!*

He would take the last can of chicken soup and set forth across the plain, and let the theropods come if they would, the big ones and the small. He did not care whether he reached the photon field or not. And then the ground quivered beneath his feet and he saw that one was already coming, the biggest one of all. Good old *Tyrannosaurus rex*. It was too late for him to run. Besides, where would he run to? "Come on, old buddy—come on! You've had my number all along!"

_____**Chapter**

_____15

WAS IT THE same tyrannosaur Sam had bested early that morning? Carpenter wondered as the huge theropod moved closer. It looked like the same one, but it did not move in quite the same way.

Instead of waddling, it jiggled up and down.

And its three-toed feet, when they struck the ground, didn't go *thump! thump!* the way feet should when they were accommodating so much weight. Instead the creature's progress was marked by a steady grinding sound.

As it walked, it roared, but the roar was atypical. It was low and soft, and not in the least ferocious.

The tyrannosaur was close enough now to afford him an excellent view of its atrophied forelegs with their talonlike fingers. Its mouth was partly open, and he was also afforded an excellent view of its teeth. The great head, perched on the trunk-thick neck, should have dismayed him, but it did not.

He was all alone in Eridahn. If he had been able to return to Earth-future, he would be all alone there too. Why should a mere dragonlike head dismay him?

He lowered his eyes and gazed with disdain at the mighty pillars of the creature's hind legs. His head came no higher than their knees.

Several yards from him the tyrannosaur came to a halt and gazed down upon him with one of its aqueous, heavy-lidded eyes. Was there enough of him to require two bites, or would one do the trick?

As he stared up at the monstrous head, the jaws parted farther. The upper one rose to an almost ninety-degree angle, and as he continued to stare, a pretty head of quite another nature appeared over the bottom row of six-inch teeth and a familiar face peered down at him.

"Miss Sands!" he gasped, and almost fell over backward.

Recovering, and, now that the threat of death was behind him, miraculously cured of his indifference to life, he walked over to the towering tyrannotank and started to pat its leg, but his hand went through the illusion field to the tread, so he patted the tread instead. "Edith, you doll you!"

"Are you all right, Mr. Carpenter?" Miss Sands called down.

"I'm fine," Carpenter said.

Another head appeared beside Miss Sands's. It was the familiar chestnut-haired head of Peter Fields, her assistant, who had been hired, at her recommendation, a month after she had been. "We're glad you're okay, Mr. Carpenter," Peter said. "I'm going to turn Edith around."

He did so and backed her up to where Sam was standing. Then he tossed a towing cable to the ground and lowered a nylon ladder from the lip of the tyrannotank's superstructure. He and Miss Sands climbed down it and proceeded to attach the cable to Edith's rear-end hitch and to a front-end hitch under Sam's snout. Carpenter lent a hand. "How'd you guys know I was in trouble? I didn't send back a can of chicken soup."

"We had a hunch," Peter Fields said. He turned to Miss Sands. "I guess we're all set now, Sandy."

"Well, let's be on our way then," Miss Sands said. She

almost looked at Carpenter. "That is, if your mission's completed, Mr. Carpenter."

Her face seemed different somehow. But it was no less lovely. If anything, it was lovelier still. He dropped his eyes to her brown field blouse. "It's completed all right, Miss Sands. And you'll never believe how it turned out."

"Oh, I wouldn't say that. Sometimes the most unbelievable things of all turn out to be true. I'll fix you something to eat, Mr. Carpenter."

She climbed agilely up the ladder. She was wearing culottes that matched her blouse and brown field boots. Peter Fields was similarly attired, except that he was wearing pants instead of culottes and a shirt instead of a blouse. Carpenter followed Miss Sands up the ladder and Peter brought up the rear. The driver's compartment was in the head, and Peter seated himself behind the wheel. Miss Sands descended the neck-ladder to the cabin. "Why don't you lie down for a while, Mr. Carpenter," Peter said. "You look bushed."

"I am, kind of," Carpenter said.

There was a bunk in the cabin. He stretched out on it. His fatigue was emotional rather than physical. Saying good-bye to Deidre and Skip and afterward seeing the tyrannosaur which had turned out to be Edith. And seeing Miss Sands again...

She had put water on to boil for coffee, and now she got a boiled ham out of the refrigerator and set it on the drainboard of the sink. He wasn't the least bit hungry, but he didn't tell her so.

Up in the driver's compartment, Peter Fields threw Edith into gear. He was a good driver, Peter Fields was, and he would rather drive than eat. And he could take a paleontologivehicle apart and put it back together blindfolded. Funny why he and Miss Sands had never gone for each other. Both were so attractive you would think they would have fallen in love with each other at first sight. Carpenter was glad they had not, but their failure to do so had not helped his cause in the least.

He wondered why neither of them had made any mention of the Space Navy ship. They must have seen it rise into the sky.

Edith was moving across the plain in a southwesterly direction toward the river and the photon field. In the rearview-scope he could see poor Sam rolling along behind her on his dead treads. He remembered how it had been that first day, and he saw himself and the kids in the driver's compartment, the kids eating sandwiches and washing them down with pop, and lovely Eridahn green with shrubs and trees and pied with pink explosions of magnolias spreading out around them, and his eyes sought out Miss Sands in an attempt to drive the poignant memory away. She was slicing ham on the drainboard. His gaze touched her booted legs and the backs of her knees which showed between her boots and her culottes, and he looked at the slenderness of her waist and raised his eyes to her copper hair and marveled at the way it flowed so softly down to her shoulders. . . . Funny the way people's hair got darker as they grew older. How even the voices of little girls underwent a subtle change. . . .

He lay motionless on the bunk. "Miss Sands," he said suddenly, "how much is 499,999,991 times 8,003,432,111?"

"400,171,598,369,111,001," Miss Sands answered.

She gave a little start. Then she resumed slicing ham.

Silence took up sovereignty in the cabin. It canceled out the faint grinding of Edith's treads and the low, soft purring of her engine. It admitted nothing into its regime except the faint sound Miss Sands's knife made as it sliced through the ham and the little clicks the blade made when it touched the drainboard.

Carpenter sat up on the bunk. He lowered his feet to the floor. Edith's air-conditioned air was cool on his face, but he found it hard to breathe.

Take a pair of lonely Martian kids who in all their lives have never known what it is like to be loved, and transport them to another planet in the clutch of terrorists and let them be rescued from an anatosaur by an Earthman who no more resembles their parents and their mentors than a dish resembles a spoon. Then put them in a reptivehicle which, for all its viability, is still a huge and delightful toy, and treat them to a camping trip and show them the first affection they have ever known. Then let them fall into the hands of the terrorists again and let the Earthman be injured rescuing them, providing them with an opportunity to show the love and courage their society

will soon rob them of. Finally, take all of this away and leave
the Earthman alone and unarmed on a hostile plain.

But 74,051,622 years! A planet whose future face they had
never seen!

It simply couldn't be! Such a fantastic journey would have
been impossible!

But *why* would it have been impossible?

Why would it have been impossible for a boy who had taken
a small time machine apart and put it back together to have
built a big one of his own? Why would it have been impossible
for him to have incorporated it in a small spaceship which, as
prince and princess, he and his sister could easily have gained
access to? Why would it have been impossible for them to have
traveled to Earth-future through space *and* time? And why
would it have been impossible for them to have found the exact
time period they had wanted when all they would have needed
to do was scan Earth's western face through the passage of the
years till the God Bless America Obelisk appeared?

They must have landed shortly after the Obelisk had been
begun. And they must have come down at night, in territory
where they could easily have hidden their ship.

They had known better than to try to make dramatic changes
in the course of events. They had known they would have to
ride with Time's waves. No doubt they had become wards of
the state—whichever state they had landed in—and later on
had been adopted. They had probably given themselves the
first names of the people they had someday hoped to be; now
they had surnames as well. They would not have had any
trouble learning English, and probably they had used their
hearrings off and on until they had mastered it. They had grown
up, and Deidre had gone to college and become a chronologist,
and afterward had gotten a job with NAPS, and then had worked
Skip in as her assistant.

They had come back to rescue Carpenter the long way around.

He sat there stunned.

Had they known before they had obtained their surnames
that they would be Miss Sands and Peter Fields? No, they could
not have known. They had only hoped that this would be so.
But whether it turned out to be so or not, their mission had

had but one objective: to rescue him and to bring him back to
A.D. 1998.

They had had to be wary of paradoxes. Miss Sands could
have done little things, such as overloading Sam with blankets
and caching bags of marshmallows in his cupboard, but neither
she nor Peter had dared to say "Mr. Carpenter, don't go to
Cretaceous-16 because you'll be badly injured there and eventually stranded." They had known they could not change what
to them had already happened, that they had to walk into Carpenter's life as strangers.

But had it really been necessary to have become such a
dedicated stranger as Miss Sands had become? Surely she could
have looked at him once in a while, have given some evidence,
at least, that she knew he was alive.

Perhaps she was ashamed of having avowed her love for
him when she had been a little girl. Grown up now, she probably thought she had behaved ridiculously.

Or was it possible that she felt the same way toward him
as he felt toward her and had been afraid all along that he might
see her love for him in her eyes before he found out who she
was?

A mist must have crept into the cabin, for Carpenter could
barely see.

Click, the blade of Miss Sands's knife went as it struck the
drainboard. *Click, click, click.*

By this time she had cut enough ham to make a bite-sized
meal for *Tyrannosaurus rex.*

"I'm—I'm not really that hungry, Miss Sands," Carpenter
said.

Miss Sands laid the knife on the drainboard.

He got to his feet. "Miss Sands," he said. She turned then,
and he saw the autumn asters of her eyes, and they were looking
at him the way they had looked at him when she was a little
girl sitting beside his bed in the Cretaceous cathedral in the
middle of the Mesozoic night. *Why, I'll bet if you told her you
loved her, she'd throw herself into your arms!*

"I love you, Pumpkin," Carpenter said.

And Miss Sands did!

About the Author

ROBERT F. YOUNG did not begin writing till his mid-thirties. He made his first sale to *Startling Stories* a few years before the magazine's demise. He has since sold to most of the science-fiction and fantasy magazines and has made sales to *Playboy* and *The Saturday Evening Post*. He has had two short-story collections published, and his novel *The Last Yggdrasill* was published by Del Rey Books in 1982.

Young was born in a small town in western New York State and has lived there all his life, other than for the three and a half years that he spent in the army during World War II and during which time he was stationed in the Solomon Islands, the Philippines, and Japan. He has worked at various jobs, carrying on his writing on a part-time basis. He is now semi-retired and writes full-time.

He is married, and his wife and he own their own house near the shore of Lake Erie. Since writing began as a hobby and took up most of his spare time, he has few others. He does considerable reading, particularly in the fields of psychology and ancient history. He enjoys writing science fiction because of the complete freedom the field gives to the imagination.

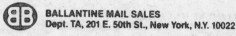